The Firework Frenzy

A Tess and Tilly Mystery

by

Kathi Daley

Tess and Tilly Cozy Mystery

The Christmas Letter

The Valentine Mystery

The Mother's Day Mishap

The Halloween House

The Thanksgiving Trip

The Saint Paddy's Promise

The Halloween Haunting

The Christmas Clause

The Puppy Project

The Wedding Plan

The Baby Plan

The Ghostly Groundskeeper

The Murder Chronicles

The Castle Caper

The Christmas Visitor

The Sleuthing Game

The Ghost Therapists

Chapter 1

"Tess Marconi?"

"Yes. I'm Tess Marconi," I answered as a tall man wearing a dark-colored uniform entered the room where I was being held for questioning.

The man paused, set a file on the table, then crossed his arms and looked down at me. He didn't speak right away, which I suspected was a tactic to make me feel uncomfortable, as if, given the situation, I could ever be comfortable. I knew from experience that when you were being interrogated, it was best not to jump in with an explanation when a question had not been asked, yet I had to fight the urge to begin blabbing. Deciding I needed a distraction, I found a black smudge on the light gray wall and focused all my attention there.

"My name is Deputy Hutchinson." the man finally broke the silence. He looked at the petite woman standing next to him. "This is my partner, Deputy Gray. Do you know why you're here?"

I redirected my attention away from the black smudge and tried to the best of my ability to look the man in the eye. "Mike, I mean Officer Thomas, told me you wanted to talk to me about Wilton Arlington. Apparently, he's dead." I took a deep breath. "Murdered, actually." I swallowed, closed my eyes, and tried to calm my racing heart. "I guess I'm a person of interest, given our recent scuffle, but I promise you that I did not kill that man."

Deputy Hutchinson sat in the chair across the table from where I'd been seated and asked to wait. I wasn't surprised that I was a suspect in the murder of the man who'd become a thorn in my side ever since my husband, Tony Marconi, and I had returned from our trip to Ashton Falls, where Tony had partnered with a tech genius, Zak Zimmerman, on an innovative project that was sure to make both men a lot of money. When I was asked to make the trip to Kalispell for the interview, I was initially surprised to find out that the sheriff was involved, but given the fact that the lead officer for my hometown of White Eagle, Montana, was my brother, Mike Thomas, I supposed I could see why there might be a certain logic in having someone other than Mike, or either of his two assistants interview me.

Hutchinson opened a file and then nodded toward Deputy Gray. This seemed to be her cue to leave the room since that was exactly what she did.

"According to this report sent to us by Officer Thomas at the time he solicited our assistance, multiple witnesses have come forward claiming to have heard you threaten to harm Mr. Arlington. In fact, three witnesses are willing to state that you said, and I quote, 'If you continue with your plans and even one animal is injured due to your total disregard for the health and wellbeing of our wild and domestic friends, I'll make sure you rue the day you ever met me.' End quote. Would you say that the witnesses we've spoken to have accurately described what was said four days ago?"

"Well, yes, but I didn't mean I was going to kill the man." I couldn't believe that Mike had shared the details of my rant with the sheriff. It really did make me look guilty. Of course, Mike did say that the only way to avoid accusations of preferential treatment was to run the investigation by the book. "I simply meant that if Arlington was the going to be the sort of man who would be willing to threaten the health and wellbeing of the wild and domestic animals we house at the animal shelter, then he wasn't the sort of man who should be in a position of power and I would use my influence as a lifelong resident of White Eagle to run the guy out of town, or at least to have him removed as president of the local Chamber of Commerce." I took a deep breath and blew it out slowly. "Look, I'm not a cold-blooded killer, but I am a passionate woman who cares deeply for the dogs, cats, and wild animals entrusted to our care. When Arlington announced that he planned to move the annual Fourth of July fireworks show from the isolated lake south of town to a small forested lake nestled at the edge of a large meadow not all that far from the animal shelter, I guess I went a little crazy. I will admit that my emotions have been elevated lately, making me even more expressive than usual, but the only thing that I've done to this point was attempt to sit down with the man and rationally explain how much harm moving the fireworks show would do to the animals we house. I politely asked him to move the show back to the original location, and when he refused, I went off on a rant." I swallowed. "I guess I said some things I shouldn't have, but I was upset and spoke without thinking about the consequences of my words."

Deputy Hutchinson opened a file and took out a piece of paper. "Is it true that you and other members of your group picketed in front of Arlington's real estate office the day after your talk with Arlington turned into a rant?"

"It's true," I admitted. "I guess I was just high on emotion and said some things I shouldn't have."

"I understand that you're expecting."

Where had that come from? Talk about an abrupt segue. I crossed my arms over the top of my sunny yellow top. "Do I show?"

"No. Not at all. I would never have known if your husband hadn't mentioned it."

"He mentioned it?"

He nodded. "I think he was trying to give me a reason to go easy on you."

"I see. You aren't going to put the details of my impending motherhood in the report you give to my brother, are you?"

"Is that a problem?"

Of course, it was a problem. Was this man as clueless as he appeared to be? "Not that it's any of your business, but Tony and I decided to wait to tell our families." I ran a hand over my stomach. It was true that I'd developed a slight bump, but I'd been wearing baggy tops, and Tony had assured me that no one could tell there was a bump beneath the top.

"Don't worry. You aren't showing. If your husband hadn't mentioned your impending motherhood, I wouldn't have known, although now that I do know, I guess that does help to explain your irrational behavior."

"I can assure you I haven't been acting irrationally," I shot back.

He raised a brow and then picked his folder up. He pulled a file out and then showed me a photo of a small group of White Eagle residents, led by yours truly, picketing outside Arlington's real estate office on Tuesday of this past week. That photo was followed by a photo of me wearing the t-shirt I'd worn the same day that showed a cartoon man holding a box of fireworks with a colorful explosion where his head should be. The caption just said: *Fireworks Kill*. Fireworks stored in Arlington's home went off later that same day, killing the man.

I suppressed a groan. "I guess I may have let my emotions get the better of me, but I didn't kill the man." I paused and looked at the file the man had been thumbing through. "I don't suppose you have anything in there that might be considered real evidence."

"The man died in a house fire. The fire investigator determined that the fire was started by fireworks stored within the home. You've been going around town wearing a t-shirt that suggests that you might end up dead if you play with fireworks."

"It was a joke." My heart began to pound. "A very, very bad joke, but a joke nonetheless."

"The explosion occurred at four thirty-seven this past Tuesday, not quite three hours after your protest was broken up and everyone was sent home."

"Yes, I know." I closed my eyes and shook my head as if trying to wake up from a bad dream.

"Can you account for your whereabouts on Tuesday at four thirty-seven?"

"After Mike broke up the protest, I was wound up, so I decided to head home, and once I arrived, I took a nap."

"Were you alone?"

"I was. Tony had gone off somewhere with our other dogs, Titan and Kody, so it was just Tilly and me."

"Tilly?"

"My dog."

"So you don't have an alibi."

I took a deep breath and then answered. "No, I guess I don't."

"How long was Tony gone?"

"I guess about four or five hours, but I'm really not sure since I'm unsure when he left home. I do know he'd left by the time I arrived."

"And what time did you get home?"

"I got home around two."

"And what time did Tony get home?"

"I guess around five-thirty."

"So, given the timeline, it's at least possible that you set the fire and still had time to make it home before Tony arrived."

"Yes," I answered. "I guess it is possible, but that isn't what happened. After Mike broke up our protest, Tilly and I headed home, and once we arrived, we went upstairs to my bedroom and took a nap. We slept for about two hours, and after we got up, we went outside and sat on the deck while we waited for Tony."

The man just looked at me. He didn't speak, and his expression was guarded.

"Look," I continued. "I know how it appears. I will admit that I picketed the man's real estate office hours before he died, and previously, I went around telling everyone that Arlington was a monster who only cared about what he wanted and didn't care a bit about the animals housed at the animal shelter. That, by the way, was true, but what wasn't true was that the guy deserved to get blown up by his own explosives. I will admit to being verbally aggressive in my campaign to get the fireworks show moved back to the original location away from the animal shelter, but once again, I want to assure you that I did not kill that man."

Suddenly, a wave of nausea gripped me. That had been happening a lot lately. My hand flew to my mouth. "I need to use the ladies' room."

"Just a few more questions."

My stomach wasn't going to wait for a few more questions, so I got up and hurried toward the corner of the room where I left my lunch.

Deputy Gray, who must have been watching, hurried into the room with a box of Kleenex® and a glass of water. "You poor thing," she said. She looked at Deputy Hutchinson. "Go and find a mop."

He left, and then Deputy Gray led me back to the table.

"I'm sorry," I said.

"Don't be. You told the man you needed to use the ladies' room, and he denied your request, so that's on him. Can I get you anything else? A mint?"

"A mint would be perfect."

She stepped out of the room and returned in under a minute, carrying ginger ale, a pack of breath mints, and a damp washcloth, which I gratefully accepted.

"How far along are you?" she asked.

"Four months."

"You really aren't showing at all. I was huge by four months."

I put my hand on my stomach. "I actually am showing, but just a little. Right now, I can hide my pregnancy with the right clothing, but I suspect those days are close to ending."

"Have you told anyone?"

"No. Not yet. Tony knows, of course, and our friends, Zak and Zoe Zimmerman, know, but they don't live in White Eagle and won't tell anyone. Tony and I were out of town when I found out that I was expecting, and we decided to wait until we were home to make an announcement, but we've been home for three weeks and still haven't gotten around to bringing anyone in on our secret." I frowned. "I'm honestly not sure why."

Deputy Gray reached out a hand and patted my knee. "You just take your time and do things in a way that feels right to you. This is your pregnancy and your timetable. Don't let anyone else tell you there is a right or a wrong way to do things."

"Thank you." I took a long drink of the ginger ale and then looked toward the two-way mirror. "Do you think Deputy Hutchinson plans to mention that I'm expecting a baby in his report?"

She shot me a look of apology. "Probably. If you want to be the one to tell your brother, I suppose you might want to do so sooner rather than later."

I supposed that filling Mike and his wife, Bree, in was inevitable. I'm not even sure why I hadn't done so before this. Bree was expecting baby number two in October and was dealing with her own pregnancy issues. I knew that she'd be thrilled that we would both have infants within months of each other and would offer me the support I needed to get through these first difficult months, so not bringing her in on the secret really made no sense. Of course, there was my mother to consider. She would likely go completely overboard with plans for another grandbaby, and I wasn't sure I was ready to deal with that.

"So what's going to happen now?" I asked Deputy Gray. "Am I going to be arrested?"

"No. We aren't going to arrest you. We really just wanted to talk to you." She leaned in close. "If you know anything that you think might help us figure out who could have decided to set off the fireworks inside Mr. Arlington's home, it would be best to tell me before Deputy Hutchinson returns."

Ah, good cop, bad cop. Classic.

"I really don't know who killed the man. Have you considered that the whole thing was an accident? I mean, the guy did have fireworks stored inside his home. I suppose it's possible that the sun might have shone through a window, reflected off a mirror, or another shiny object, which might have become hot enough to cause a flame."

"We did consider the idea that the fireworks might have ignited due to a situation such as the one you've just described, but we have additional evidence that suggests that the fireworks were ignited by using a fuse."

"A fuse? Inside the man's home?"

"The fireworks weren't actually inside the house. They were kept in a windowless storage shed attached to the main structure but accessed from the home's exterior. The investigator assigned to determine the point of origin and cause of the fire found what remained of a fuse that ran from the house toward the forest beyond the home. At this point, it appears that someone intentionally set off the fireworks."

"Why would anyone intentionally create such a huge explosion?"

Deputy Gray looked up as Deputy Hutchinson returned to the room. Deputy Gray was the one who answered, but I could feel Deputy Hutchinson watching my face.

"I can't be sure why the person did things the way he or she did," Deputy Gray began, "but it does seem at least possible that the use of fireworks as the murder weapon was both symbolic and intentional."

Okay. This wasn't good. If I didn't know for a fact that I had not killed that man, even I would suspect me. "I've told you what I know. Am I free to go?" I asked.

Gray looked at Hutchinson, who nodded. I'd be willing to bet a week's pay that Deputy Hutchinson had been in the other room, watching from behind the two-way mirror the entire time Deputy Gray and I spoke. There was no way it had taken him this long to find a mop.

"You're free to go," Deputy Gray said. "And thank you for taking the time out of your busy day to come in."

"I didn't get the impression that this interview was optional, but you're welcome."

"If you think of anything else, please do call me," Deputy Gray said, handing me her card before standing up to walk me out.

Tony was waiting for me in the front office. I was never so happy to see anyone as I was to see him standing there waiting to take me home.

"Let's get out of here," I said as Tony put his arm around my shoulders and led me to his truck.

Once Tony had loaded me into the truck and made sure I was buckled up tight, I started to cry.

"What is it?" he asked. "Are you okay?"

"I'm fine. It's just my stupid hormones and maybe a delayed reaction to stress. Let's get out of here. The sooner I'm safely home with the animals, the happier I'll be."

Tony pulled away from the curb. "Do you want to talk about it?"

"Not really."

"Okay, I'll drive and let you process, but if you need to talk, I'm ready to listen."

I nodded, and just as he promised he would, Tony drove toward White Eagle without making a sound.

Once we arrived at our mountain home on the lake, the shakiness I'd been experiencing began to subside. Tilly, who I imagined sensed my distress, glued herself to my side while my cats, Tang and Tinder, said hello and then returned to what they'd been doing.

"Can I get you anything else?" Tony asked after he settled me on a padded lounge chair on the patio with a tall glass of herbal iced tea, a small pillow, a throw blanket, even though it wasn't cold, and a book I'd already read and wouldn't likely read again.

"I have everything I need," I said to the man I loved beyond all else. I set the book aside. "I think I'm just going to close my eyes and try to relax."

"I know I asked you this before, but are you ready to talk about it?" he asked.

"I do want to talk to you about it, but not yet. Is there any of that cobbler left from dinner last night?"

"There is."

"I'll take a piece. And maybe add a small scoop of ice cream on the side."

Once Tony had dashed toward the house, I allowed the remaining unshed tears I'd been suppressing to flow freely. I understood why Tony was worried about me. Given the circumstances involving my possible arrest, he'd worry about me no matter my state, but ever since we'd taken the home pregnancy test and confirmed our impending parenthood, he'd been treating me like a fragile flower. At first, that bothered me, but Zoe, who had been through it twice before, counseled me to relax and enjoy the pampering. Zoe admitted that when she was pregnant with the couple's first child, she, too, had been annoyed by the hovering but decided to stop fighting it. Zoe also shared that once she learned to let her husband cater to her every whim, she realized she actually enjoyed it quite a bit.

After Tony brought me my cobbler, he sat on the lounge chair next to the one I was sitting on. I could tell he wanted to know how my interview had gone and had been patiently waiting for me to be ready to talk about it. Truth be told, I would have preferred to talk about almost anything else, but if he'd been the one interviewed by the sheriff's office, I'd be dying to know how it went, so I decided not to leave him in suspense.

"The interview went fine," I said, stabbing at a plump cherry. "As you know, Arlington died in a house fire after the fireworks he had stored in his home ignited and created a huge explosion. Also, as you know, I've been going around town wearing a t-shirt depicting a cartoon man holding a box of fireworks as his head is blown off by those fireworks." I took another bite of the cobbler. "I know you warned me on more than one occasion that the t-shirt was in poor taste and that while you understood my duress over the prospect of the community fireworks show being held so close to the animal shelter, you also thought I might want to take a step back from my very public displays of outrage." I stabbed at another cherry. "I guess you were right about that."

"So, does the deputy you spoke to really think you might have killed that man?"

I took a bite of the ice cream and allowed it to dissolve slowly in my mouth. "Deputy Hutchinson does consider me to be a person of interest, but the reality is that he has nothing to tie me to the murder scene. I won't go so far as to say that I'm off the hook, but now that he's interviewed me, I suspect they've shuffled my file down toward the bottom of the pile."

Tony blew out a long breath. "That's good. I know that there's no way you could have done such a thing, and no one who knows you would believe that you could have killed a man, but there are going to be rumors. I mean, in a roundabout way, you did suggest that the man might deserve what he got should he actually end up getting blown up by his fireworks show."

I groaned. "I know. The whole thing was in poor taste. I really don't know what got into me. When we got home from Ashton Falls, and I found out that this guy was planning to move the fireworks show to the lake near the animal shelter, I went crazy. It was like my rage took over, and I lost control of my common sense." I took another bite of the cobbler. "While I was sitting there in the interrogation room, it actually occurred to me that if I was the one investigating the man's death, I'd suspect me as well, and with good reason."

Tony reached over and took my hand in his. "I know you've been sensitive to my natural instinct to hover a bit since we found out about the baby, and I want you to know that I'm not trying to invade your space, but I do think that it might be best if we hang out here at the house for a while."

I took one look at Tony's face and felt awful. He looked so nervous. Like he was afraid that I was going to bite his head off for even suggesting a course of action. Had I really been that over-the-top reactive? I guess maybe I had been.

I smiled. "I think that might be a good idea. At least for a few days."

A look of relief washed over his face. "Maybe we can start working on the flower boxes. We usually have them finished by this point in the summer, but between our trip and everything that's been going on since we've been home, we haven't even started yet."

"It would be nice to have them done by the Fourth of July party."

"Are you sure we shouldn't just call your mom and cancel the party?"

"The party she's been planning since February?" I asked.

"I know your mom is really invested in the whole thing, but if we tell her about the baby, maybe she'll be so happy that she won't care."

"No," I said decisively. "I'm not ready to tell Mom about the baby yet, but we do need to tell Mike and Bree. It sounds as if Deputy Hutchinson plans to mention my pregnancy in his report, which we both know Mike will see."

Tony hung his head. "I'm sorry that I mentioned it. I know we agreed to wait until you felt ready, and it wasn't my secret to tell."

I squeezed his hand. "It's fine. I know that by telling him, you hoped the guy would go easy on me, and maybe he did. And," I added, "I guess that it really is time to start filling a few people in. We'll start with Mike and Bree and take it from there."

"Maybe we should invite Mike and Bree to dinner," Tony suggested.

I nodded. "Yeah, it would be a good idea to tell them sooner rather than later. Besides, I need to ask Mike a few things about Arlington's murder case."

"I thought you were going to stay out of it."

"I said I'd stay home, but I never said I'd stay out of it," I countered.

Tony just groaned, but he didn't argue.

"I also need to confirm that Mike, Bree, you, and I have our stories straight regarding Uncle Garret. Mom is going to be looking for a lie. I honestly suspect that she's beginning to question our story. Although, it would be quite a stretch for her to believe that Uncle Garret is actually Dad, even if her senses are telling her that's the case."

"So does that mean we're going to stick with the story of Uncle Garret being overseas for his job?" Tony asked.

"I think that's the only excuse she might accept. If we simply tell her that Uncle Garret's busy that day or he needs to work, she'll want details, and once she has those, she'll try to unravel any argument we come up with. Asking the man to fly home from Europe isn't a reasonable request. I'm sure she'll understand that."

"And what about Thanksgiving and Christmas? Now that your mom has met Uncle Garret, she isn't going to let this go."

I leaned my head against the pillow and blew out a long breath. "I know, and, at this point, I'm not sure what to do, but I guess it isn't just up to us. Mike seems to be invested in the idea of trying to bring Dad back into our lives, which is a feeling I understand, but I don't see how that would work. Even if we tell Mom that Dad's death was a mistake and that he really is alive, the reason he faked his death in the first place is still going to exist. Dad faked his death to protect Mom, Mike, and me from the life he'd chosen, and, as far as I know, nothing has really changed on that front since he's still buried deep in that life. The three of us are no longer the only individuals who might be in danger because of our affiliation with Dad. If someone really wanted to hurt Dad, then hurting Ella, Mike and Bree's son once he's born, or our baby once he or she is born is a real possibility. I really don't see a way to resolve this."

"I guess you make a good point that it would be best if your dad stayed dead," Tony agreed. "Of course, for that to really happen, your dad needs to stay away, Mike needs to let him, and we need to find a way to kill Uncle Garret off so your mom stops trying to make him part of the family."

"Trying to figure all of that out is giving me a headache. I agree with your suggestion to invite Mike and Bree to dinner. Once they're here, we can share the news that we're expecting a baby, and then the four of us can address the Uncle Garret issue. Maybe we can even find a solution."

"I'll call Mike right now," Tony said. "You just sit here and relax. Is there anything else I can get for you?"

"No. I'm fine."

"What time should I tell them to come if, in fact, they're able to come to dinner?"

"Any time is fine. I was thinking about a nap, but I think I'll skip it today. In fact, after you finish inside, come back out, and we'll start talking about the color schemes for the planter boxes. I need something ordinary to take my mind off all the non-ordinary things that are stomping their way through my head."

"Like your dad?"

"Like my dad, Arlington's death, and a plan to not only solve his death but to get the fireworks show moved back to its original location before someone decides that it's too late to make a change."

"There's time. I'll go call Mike, and then I'll grab a notepad and pen and come back out." He looked toward the crystal blue lake. "It really is a nice day. I'm going to miss this when we move."

"If we move," I said.

He looked at me. "If we move." With that, he walked away.

One of the many discussions Tony and I had been having since we'd first decided to start trying for a baby was our living situation. Being all the way up on the mountain worked for the two of us since Tony worked from home, and I worked when it suited me, but once we had children and those children began to go to school, we would need to be closer to town. And not just for school but for after-school activities, playdates with friends, and all the other social commitments children seemed to be involved with these days. While I agreed with Tony that it made sense to live in town to be close to everything, I found myself resisting the idea. I wasn't sure why. Before moving in with Tony, I'd been happy in my little cabin, which was located close to town. If we found the right place, I was pretty sure I'd be happy again. Yet, when I thought about giving up our lakeside retreat, it made me sad. I supposed it would take some time for me to get used to all the changes, but I was excited about bringing a mini-Tony or a mini-me into the world, so maybe once he or she arrived, everything I felt I was losing would simply cease to matter.

Chapter 2

I spent a full thirty minutes rehearsing my announcement to Mike and Bree that Tony and I were expecting without making them angry that we hadn't told them right away, but it was all for naught since the moment Mike and Bree walked into the house, Bree approached me and cradled my bump with her hands.

"You are pregnant," she accused.

I looked at Tony, pleading for help.

"We are," Tony said. "In fact, bringing you in on the secret was the main reason we asked you over tonight."

"But you must be at least three months along." Bree crossed her arms over her chest, resting them on her stomach. "Why didn't you tell me before this?"

"We were in Ashton Falls when we found out, and we planned to tell you when we got back, but things have been a bit hectic," I said.

Bree opened her mouth as if to argue when Mike reached out a hand, shook Tony's, and congratulated him. He sent Bree a meaningful look that had her closing her mouth and reaching out to hug me instead of chastising me further.

"I'm so happy for you both," Mike said as he came over to hug me while Bree turned her attention to Tony.

"Thank you both," I said. "Tony and I are so happy. Terrified, but happy."

Bree laughed and then made a comment about remembering the terror she felt during her first pregnancy when she realized that she was actually going to have to carry and deliver a baby. Poor Bree had had a difficult time when she was pregnant with Ella, but luckily, this pregnancy had been going smoother. Of course, smoother for Bree was still pretty bad. I guessed some people were genetically inclined to suffer all the side effects while others breezed through.

"Speaking of Ella, where is she?" I asked.

"Your mom and Sam took her for the day. Mike had to work, and I wasn't feeling well when I first woke up, so Mike called your mom, and Sam came by to pick her up. We'll pick her up on our way home."

"It really is nice of Sam to help out the way he does," I said.

Bree agreed.

"So when exactly are you due?" Bree asked.

"Just before Christmas."

"So you're further along than I thought." Bree looked me up and down. "You really aren't showing at all with that full top on. I assume that you haven't told anyone else."

"No." I decided not to mention the fact that Zak and Zoe knew. "Just the two of you. I imagine I'll have to tell Mom sooner rather than later, but I hoped I could put it off until after the Fourth of July party. I'm afraid that she'll decide to parade me around sharing my news with all our friends if she knows I'm expecting, and I think I need to work up to that."

"On the one hand, it's true that your mom is going to go crazy when she hears the news, but on the other hand, if your mom knows about the baby, she's less apt to be as demanding as she's been up to this point. I can't imagine why she's been so hyped up over this party, but I have noticed that she's been riding you and Tony fairly hard."

"I think Mom is dealing with thoughts of mortality that she hasn't really dealt with to this point," I said. "Not that she's old by any means, but she is getting older, and I think that has caused her to look back at her life and deal with some of her regrets."

"I guess you did mention something about that when we spoke after you returned from Lake Tahoe this past winter," Bree admitted. She laughed. "I swear that I'm not sure what's worse. Pregnancy brain with its total randomness of what I do and don't remember, or the gassy stomach that seems to be my constant companion. How's your stomach been?"

"Mostly fine." I could have shared my bout with nausea at the sheriff's office but decided against it since I wasn't sure I wanted to get into the whole murder enigma until after dinner.

"I hope that my choice of lasagna for dinner won't be too spicy for you," Tony said to Bree. "I can make you something else if you prefer."

"I do love your lasagna. I think it will be fine. While I'll miss having wine with the Italian meal, I'll settle for water."

"I actually have non-alcoholic mojitos that I thought all of us can try," Tony said. "They're light and refreshing and made with all-natural ingredients, and, best of all, they're low in sugar and, as the name indicates, non-alcoholic."

"That sounds nice," Bree said.

Tony had undeniably gone out of his way to ensure that I never felt left out. He liked his wine but had been choosing something non-alcoholic to drink with me ever since we found out that we were expecting.

Once we were all settled on the patio with our beverages, I decided that it was time to bring up the Uncle Garret problem.

"Telling Mom that Uncle Garret is overseas for work will give us a reason for his absence at the Fourth of July party, but it isn't a long-term solution," I pointed out. "Tony and I have discussed this quite a bit, and the only solution we can come up with is to tell Dad to leave and not come back and then to tell Mom that something happened to Uncle Garret."

"I understand the dilemma, but I, for one, am not okay with that," Mike said. "Ever since Dad started stopping by early in the morning to chat with me and play with Ella, I honestly feel as if I have a father. We've grown closer than we ever were when he lived at home. Dad was gone most of the time and emotionally distant when he was home during the years when we were growing up. Now, we chat, and I feel like we're really getting to know each other. Did you know he loves baseball and can answer almost any baseball-related trivia question you can come up with?"

"No, I didn't know that," I admitted.

"He loves to camp and fish. He can speak seven languages fluently and understands more than that."

"Wow. That is impressive," I admitted.

"Dad has had to make hard choices in his life in order to protect us, but I can see that he's at a point where he's looking back on those choices with regret," Mike continued. "He loves spending time with Ella and is extremely excited about having a second grandchild. I'm sure that once Dad finds out you're expecting a baby, too, he'll be almost as excited as Mom when you tell her. Dad deserves to know us, and we deserve to know him. I'm not going to ask him to walk away. There has to be another way."

"Okay, then what other way is there?" I asked. I sat forward and looked Mike in the eye. "I understand how you feel. I do. I feel the same way. But I don't want to put either of our families in harm's way by trying to maintain a relationship with a man who a lot of deplorable people want dead."

I was happy that Mike and Dad had connected in such a meaningful way, but I could see that their new relationship was going to complicate things. When Tony and I had first found out that Dad was still alive and that his death in a fiery crash had been faked, we'd made the decision not to tell Mike and Bree what we'd found. When Mike eventually found out, he'd been so mad. I really thought it might ruin our relationship, but he'd found a way to forgive me. In the beginning, even after Mike and Bree knew the truth about Dad, Dad chose to communicate with Tony rather than Mike or me. I knew that hurt Mike, but now it sounded like it was Mike who Dad had chosen to trust, and I was confident that meant more to Mike than Dad would ever know.

"And it's not just the danger to our families," I added. "It sounds as if you and Dad have had some quality breakfasts together, but his being in town, even if he is careful, is always a risk, and the more times he shows up, the more chance there is that Mom is going to find out the truth."

"Maybe we should tell Mom the truth," Mike suggested. "It seems the real problem here is Mom's insistence on including Uncle Garret in family gatherings, which we all realize is a dangerous path. But if she knew the truth, Dad could stay in the background, and we could be a family again."

"I really do understand where you're coming from, Mike. But just because Dad isn't really dead, that doesn't mean we can be a family again. Mom has moved on. She's with Sam now, and Sam is good for Mom. He's stable and seems to put her needs above his own. Dad was never there for her like that, even when they were together. If we tell Mom that Dad is alive, all that can serve to do is mess up the good thing she currently has."

Tony joined in for the first time. "Not to counter my gorgeous wife, but I'm not sure that knowing the truth will affect your mom's relationship with Sam the way you think it will. Based on my observations, your mother has moved on. If she found out that your dad is alive, I suppose there would need to be a period of adjustment, but I'm not sure that finding out that her dead husband is an international spy who is very much alive would impact her relationship with Sam in the long run. She's good with Sam. I think she knows what she has, and I don't think she'd walk away from it easily."

"It is true that Dad seems to be okay with Sam, and Sam seems to be okay with Dad," Mike said.

"Maybe," I agreed. "But telling Mom is still a huge risk."

"We may not have a choice," Mike said. "I wasn't going to mention this just yet, but the last time Dad stopped by, he mentioned to me that he'd heard that Mom had been going around telling everyone about her dead husband's lookalike brother. Dad is afraid that the rumors will get back to those who want to do him harm, and the very people he died to draw away from White Eagle are going to come poking around to see if the rumor of this lookalike brother is true."

Wasn't this the exact case I'd been trying to make earlier? I wanted to say as much, but I resisted the urge. The truth of the matter was that it was unlikely that Dad would ever be able to outrun his past, and as long as there were people who wanted to do him harm, our families would be at risk as well.

"How to deal with your father and the decisions that will need to be made in order to protect our families going forward is not going to be solved here tonight, but it sounds like we need to talk to your mom no matter what course of action we take with your father," Tony said.

"I think talking to Mom is our best and maybe only course of action," Mike agreed.

Even though I was disenchanted with the idea for many reasons, it did sound like we might not have as many options as I'd initially thought we had.

"Let's talk to Sam before we do anything," I suggested. "Sam knows the whole story, and he's familiar with the people who might be looking for

Dad. He cares about us, and he cares about Mom. I think he's likely in the best position to help us figure this whole thing out."

Once we'd agreed to talk to Sam, Tony went into the kitchen to take the lasagna out of the oven and toss the salad. After the garlic bread was browned, he set the table and invited us all to have a seat. I still wanted to ask Mike about Wilton Arlington's murder case, and I suspected he wanted to ask me about my interview, although based on Bree's actions when she first arrived, I was willing to bet he'd already seen the report.

"So, about Wilton Arlington's murder," I said once we'd eaten, the table had been cleared, and Tony had settled us all on the patio with coffee or herbal tea.

"I was wondering when you were going to bring that up," Mike said.

"I'm sure you know that I have a vested interest in making certain the actual killer is caught. Agent Hutchinson said very little about what might or might not have been discovered during the series of interviews you've been conducting. Do you mind filling me in?"

Mike hesitated, but only for a minute. The two of us had worked together many times in the past, and with Tony's help, we'd managed to amass one heck of a close rate. While he might need to be a little more careful about what he said to me since I was, after all, a suspect, I actually doubted that he'd cut me out completely.

Mike responded. "Arlington was an outspoken man with strong opinions and an unreserved way about him. It seems that most residents of White Eagle either loved or hated him. The man was the sort to strike a nerve as he moved through his agenda of projects, which meant that he made as many loyal followers as he did enemies along the way."

"So I wasn't the only one talking smack about the guy?"

Mike glanced at me with a lopsided grin. "No. You undeniably weren't the only one talking smack about the guy. I will admit that you spoke a bit more loudly than most, but there are others who seem to have reason to have wanted him dead."

"Does anyone stand out?" I asked.

"I have a list which Frank, Gage, and I are slowly whittling away at. I've either personally spoken to or had Deputy Hutchinson speak to almost everyone on the list by this point, and while there are a handful of residents who seem to have had more of a motive than others, I haven't settled on anyone as the prime suspect in this case." Mike referred to his two assistants, Frank Hudson and Gage Wilson.

"So what now?" I asked.

"I've been waiting for a few reports from the crime lab. A couple of the reports I was waiting on came in today, while a few others have been promised to me no later than tomorrow. Once I have reports dealing with any physical evidence that was found at the scene, which wasn't a lot given the intensity of the fire, and the final report from the medical examiner, I guess I'll meet with the guys, and we'll take all the data we have and try to come up with a course of action."

"Can I help?" I asked.

"No," Mike and Tony said at the same time.

"But…" I countered.

"You are still a suspect," Mike reminded me. "Unless you want to end up in jail, you will stay well away from any of this."

"Tony wants me to stay home until you unravel everything," I said.

"That would be perfect," Mike agreed. "In fact, other than coming into town with Tony for essential things like doctor's appointments, my recommendation would be for you to maintain a low profile. Even though I went out of my way to bring in an outside perspective when it came to processing you as a suspect, there will still be people who will assume that I'm giving you preferential treatment. And not just preferential treatment, since there will be those who assume I'll do everything I can to cover it up even if you are guilty."

I knew that I'd put Mike in a formidable situation. Since I really didn't want to make things any harder on him, I agreed to stay home even though I very much doubted that my promise to him was one I was going to be able to keep if this case dragged on for longer than a day or two.

Chapter 3

After a very long night of tossing and turning and then going over everything in my mind a million times, I was more than ready to take control of things and do some digging of my own. Of course, I had promised Mike that I'd stay home, and if I was both going to dig around and stay home, I would need Tony's help, so the first order of business, I decided, was to sweet talk my very attentive husband into doing a search I knew he was not going to want to do. My natural instinct was to jump right in with my request, but when he greeted me with breakfast in bed, followed by the suggestion of a trip into town to buy the flowers we needed for our planter boxes, I decided to go along with his plan, and, hopefully, once he'd begun to fully relax I'd be able to bring up my concerns and ideas in a way that might actually gain his attention and cooperation.

"I was thinking of red, white, and blue flowers since we are having the Fourth of July party at our home on the fourth, but we did that same color scheme last year, so I feel inclined to mix it up a bit. I noticed the nursery had California poppies in both orange and red when I was in for some mulch the other day. I thought the orange and red colored poppies mixed with a deep purple or dark blue flower, accented with something lighter, maybe yellow, would look nice."

"That does sound nice," I agreed. I had to admit that I wasn't as invested in the flowers as I might have been had there not been so much going on in my life, but I did want to support Tony in his plan to distract me from Arlington's murder at least on the surface, so I decided to wait to broach the subject and ask for his help. "I really liked those purple flowers you used a couple of years ago."

"Angelonia. Or maybe viola. We'll look at both, and you can point out which purple flowers you're thinking of."

Tony and I continued to discuss flowers all the way to the nursery. Even though flowers were really the furthest thing from my mind, after a bit of idle chit-chat with the man I loved, I did find that it was beginning to help me relax. By the time we'd made the trip to the nursery, walked around in the moist flower tent for at least an hour, made our selections, and headed toward the checkout, I was more than ready for a nap. I still hadn't decided if afternoon naps to alleviate pregnancy fatigue were a luxury or an annoying distraction, but on the rare occasions when I'd skipped the nap, I'd only ended up being moody later in the day.

"Hap, Hattie," I greeted one of my favorite couples who just happened to get in line behind us. Hap Hollister owned the hardware and home supply store, and Hattie owned the best bakery in town. I glanced down at their cart, which was overflowing with annuals. "It looks like you had the same idea we did."

"Hap made new planter boxes for the back of the house," Hattie informed me. "We meant to get them planted earlier in the season, but here we are well into June, and we're just getting around to it."

"I see you went with pink, purple, and white. Tony and I did that color pallet one year and really enjoyed it." I glance down at our cart. "This year, I was in the mood for something a bit bolder."

"I like the bright colors," Hap said. "They really stand out."

"I thought so," I agreed. "I think your flowers are going to be lovely as well. I'll need to stop by for a peek after you get them planted."

"Anytime," Hap said. "I've missed you and Tilly. It seems like it's been a while since you've stopped by the store to say hi."

"Tony and I were out of town for over a month," I reminded him. "And while we've been back for three weeks, I guess you can say that things have grown somewhat complicated."

"I heard you had a bit of trouble. Been hoping I'd have the chance to ask you about it."

I responded to Hap's statement. "I imagine everyone who has heard about Arlington's death is wondering if I did it. Just so you know, I didn't."

"I never thought that for a minute." Hap huffed out a sentence so firm as to leave no doubt about his sincerity. "Of course, that doesn't mean that others will give you the same benefit of the doubt. I hope those who supported Arlington aren't making things harder on you than they need to be."

"As if anyone would believe for even a single moment that this sweet child could kill a man," Hattie agreed.

"I agree with that fully," Hap supported his wife, "but we both know how the rumor mills seem to create an implied truth that sometimes takes on a life of its own."

"I'm fine. Really," I assured the sweet older man. "I've had to go to the sheriff's office in Kalispell to answer some questions, but other than fully cooperating with Mike and his team, I'm staying out of it." I glanced at Tony. "My big teddy bear of a husband has been taking good care of me, so neither of you needs to worry."

"I'm glad to hear that," Hap said. "I know I've said as much before, but you're like the daughter I never had. I don't know what I'd do if something happened to you."

Tony put his arm around my shoulders. "I'm keeping her close, so there's no need to worry."

"As I said, I've missed having you pop in at the store, but I guess it might be best for you to keep a low profile until Mike catches the actual killer," Hap said.

"I ran into your mother this morning, and she mentioned the Fourth of July party," Hattie said, effectively changing the subject. "I guess that's still on."

"It's still on," I said. "And when you and Hap come by for the party, you'll be able to see the planter boxes that Tony and I are working on."

Tony and I continued to chat with Hap and Hattie until we reached the checkout register. We paid for our flowers and then headed out to the truck. I was sorry that Hap had been so worried about me but somewhat flattered as well. He was a good friend, and I needed to do a better job of staying in contact with him now that I was only doing my mail route on an as-needed basis.

"I really enjoyed today," I said as we drove back up the mountain.

Tony turned and smiled at me. "Me too. Planting our flowers every summer is one of my favorite things that we do together. Do you remember our first spring as a couple?"

I smiled. I did remember that first spring. On the one hand, it felt like a lifetime ago in many ways, but on the other hand, it seemed like just yesterday.

"After you finished planting flowers in your yard, you built planter boxes for my cabin and brought them by as a surprise. I returned home from my route to find that my entire deck had been transformed into a flower garden. I couldn't believe you had invested so much time and effort to make everything perfect for me."

"It was worth it when I saw the smile on your face."

I leaned my head on his shoulder and let my thoughts take me back. By the time Tony was done, not only did I have flowers but freshly painted patio furniture as well.

"Whatever happened to the swing I had on the deck at my cabin?" I asked. I didn't remember giving it away when I moved in with Tony, but I didn't remember seeing it since then.

"It's in the shed. Unfortunately, it was damaged in the move, so my plan was to fix it and then refinish it, but I guess it must not have been a priority since I never got around to doing what I had planned to do. The rockers that were on your deck are in the shed as well. I've been picturing sitting in one of those chairs watching the sunset as I rock our baby ever since I found out we were having a baby."

I loved the fact that Tony spent time daydreaming about our baby. I supposed I'd spent some time thinking about the baby as well. But if I was honest with myself, I'd have to admit that most of my daydreams had to do with problems to be met and tasks to be completed, while it seemed that Tony spent time thinking about such things as rocking our child as the day ended and the sun slipped behind the mountain.

"Once we're finished in the yard, I guess we might want to start thinking about a nursery," I said.

Tony reached his right hand out and took mine in his as he continued to drive with his left hand.

"I know we have a nursery for Ella, but I'd like our baby to have his or her own crib and furniture," I added. "I've been thinking about updating the paint and décor as well. I want the room to be his or hers rather than a generic room."

"I'm glad you said that since I've started digging around online, looking for ideas. Of course, knowing if we're having a boy or girl would be helpful."

"We can find out at our next doctor's appointment if you want. I wasn't sure if I wanted to know at first, but the further along I get and the more I begin to think of the bump beneath my baggy top as a baby, the more I realize that I do want to know if he or she is a boy or girl." I turned my head and looked at Tony. "I assume that it's okay with you if we find out the gender of our baby."

"It is. Like you, the more real the idea becomes to me, the more of an urge I have to start to imagine what our baby will be like."

Tony pulled onto the private road leading out to our house.

"Do you have a preference?" I asked.

"Not at all. Do you?"

I paused to consider the question. "No, at least I don't think so. During the years leading up to conceiving a child, I've thought about how it would be to have both a boy and a girl. Along the way, I guess that I have found myself leaning in one direction or the other, but now that the time to find out is actually here, I find that I'm fine either way."

"I know we've been calling the baby Kiwi due to his or her approximate size when we gave him or her the name, but once we find out if we're having a boy or a girl, I guess we can decide on a real name."

"Or we can choose now and select a name that would be gender-neutral," I said. "Something like Jordan, Parker, Riley, Dylan, Sawyer, or Peyton."

Tony slowed and pulled into our drive. "I really like that idea. In fact, I like all the names you suggested. I'll start planting the flowers while you take a nap. Once we've finished the planting, we'll sit on our patio, look out at our lake, enjoy a non-alcoholic beverage, and begin to imagine who our baby might be."

As much as I really did want to jump in and get Arlington's murder solved, somewhere between buying flowers, taking a walk down memory lane, and starting to create mental images of the child Tony and I would welcome in five short months, I decided that murder and suspects could wait another day. Not that I wasn't invested in the outcome of the investigation, but Tony and I had been going what felt like a hundred miles an hour for months. First, there had been the push to get his game ready for the convention in Tahoe, then came the offer to develop new software with Zak Zimmerman, which had led to a month-long stay in Ashton Falls, followed by my campaign to stop Arlington from moving the annual Fourth of July fireworks show to the lake near the animal shelter, and finally to my status as a suspect in the man's murder. While Tony and I had been happy when I found out that I was pregnant with our first child, and hugs and kisses had been exchanged all around, today was the first time we'd actually stopped to process the whole thing as a couple. Sure, we'd talked about issues such as when to tell people, where we'd live, and which OBGYN I should make an appointment with, but we'd never really stopped to imagine how it would be when Tony and I actually became a family of three.

Chapter 4

The weekend had been absolutely perfect. Despite the fact I'd been determined to dig into Arlington's murder from the moment I woke up on Saturday, a couple of days spent with Tony making plans and dreaming about our family was exactly what I needed. I still wanted to get the fireworks show moved, and I still wanted Arlington's actual killer found so that those members of the community who might wonder if maybe I hadn't done it could have their doubts put to rest, but since I was carrying precious cargo, I did need to be extra careful. That didn't mean I couldn't work to accomplish both tasks, but instead of trying to find a way to go around Tony, I planned to elicit his help.

"I'd like to drop in on the mayor today," I said. "I texted with Aspen yesterday to ask how things were going with the new training program at the animal shelter, and she mentioned that while the training was going well, there was still a lot of stress all around over the fireworks show, which, as far as she knew, was still on. I know I promised to stay away from the whole Wilton Arlington murder thing, but that doesn't mean I can't work on getting the fireworks show moved before it's too late." I referred to Aspen Wood, the wildlife specialist Brady Baker, the local veterinarian and animal shelter owner, had hired to help him develop the wildlife side of what originally had been a domestic dog and cat shelter when I'd taken a step back and merged into more of an on-call position.

Tony didn't answer right away. I suspected that he hoped I'd simply stay home, plant flowers, and allow the rest of the world to run itself, but I also suspected he knew that yesterday was an anomaly and it was unlikely I'd be spending too many days doing nothing about the issues I cared about.

"I'd really like you to come with me if you have time," I added.

The tension in his expression softened a bit. "Okay. Maybe we'll head into town after breakfast. We can drop in on the mayor and take care of a few errands I have on my list as well."

"That sounds perfect. We'll bring Tilly and stop by and say hi to Hap while we're out. When we spoke to him yesterday, I could tell he misses our daily visits."

"Okay. I'm going to head upstairs to change my shirt while you finish eating."

Dropping in on the mayor without an appointment was a strategic risk. On the one hand, Tony and I both felt that if we called ahead for an appointment, the mayor would likely anticipate the reason for our visit and put us off, while if we just dropped in, he'd likely be forced to speak to us. On the other hand, it was possible that the mayor wasn't even in his office today, and if that was the case, our trip into town would have been a waste of time. Of course, it was a good day for a drive, and since Tony had errands he wanted to attend to, maybe the trip wouldn't be a waste either way.

When we arrived at the mayor's office, we noticed the man was sitting behind his desk. His secretary was away, so Tony poked his head into his office through the open doorway and asked to speak to the man. I supposed the guy could have told Tony that he was on his way to a meeting or needed to take a call, but Tony and I had both done a ton of favors for the mayor and the town in the past, so when Tony asked to speak to him, he waved us in.

"So what can I do for you today?" he asked.

"I'm here to discuss the fireworks show. Again," I said. "As you know, I have grave concerns about moving the fireworks to the little lake near the animal shelter. I know I've spoken to you about this before, and you pushed me off on Wilton Arlington, but Arlington is no longer in the picture, so now I'm back to talk to you."

Tony sent me a look that made me realize that my approach might have been a bit more aggressive than it needed to be.

"What Tess means," Tony said, "is that now that Wilton Arlington is no longer running things, we felt it was best to bring our concerns directly to you."

"You want the fireworks show moved back to the lake south of town."

Tony nodded. "Yes. We feel that the new location chosen by Arlington is too close to the animal shelter and will likely do harm to the animals housed there."

"The Chamber of Commerce is sponsoring the event, and they are using their own funds to pay for the fireworks, so I've been trying to defer to their decisions on the matter, but if you feel it is a real problem, I guess I can step in."

"That would be great," I grinned.

"Of course, I may need a tiny favor in exchange for my interference in this matter."

"Favor?" I asked.

"Grandy Brown is moving out of the state."

Grandy Brown was a long-time White Eagle resident who often helped with community events in the same way that Tony and I did.

"Yes, I'd heard that," I responded.

"Grandy was supposed to chair the Halloween event. I'll need to replace him."

"And you want us to do it?" I asked.

He nodded.

I could see that Tony was about to turn him down, but I jumped in and agreed to take on the task before Tony could voice his opinion. It was true that I'd be seven months pregnant by Halloween, but pregnant wasn't incapacitated, and I'd have Tony to help me.

"Excellent," the mayor said. "It's going to help a lot that you've worked with Tim and Tom in the past."

"Tim Rivers and Tom Masters?" I asked. Tim and Tom were the hosts of the popular TV show *Ghost Therapy*. They'd been in town three years ago to offer therapy to the ghost who purportedly lived on the Franktown Estate. They were nice guys. A bit kooky but nice.

"Apparently, the team is interested in the Stonewall Estate this time. Grandy worked out a deal similar to the one you worked out with them three years ago. Now that Grandy is moving, we need someone who knows the ropes to oversee the entire thing. I guess I'm lucky I have you."

"Yeah, lucky," I said.

Tony had a frown on his face, but I could see that he was relieved by the way things worked out when I asked the mayor to give me something in writing that said that the fireworks show would officially be moved back to the original location by the end of the day, and he agreed.

"You know that you're going to be very pregnant by the time Halloween rolls around," Tony pointed out after we left the mayor's office and stepped out into the warm sunshine.

"I know, but my being a little uncomfortable will be worth not having the shelter's animals subjected to the fireworks. We've run the Halloween event many times in the past, and we've worked with Tim and Tom, so there is no reason to think things won't go smoothly."

"Do things ever go smoothly?"

I took Tony's hand in mine. "Not so far, but there's always a first time for everything." I glanced down at Tilly. "Let's take Tilly to see Hap, and then we'll head to the animal shelter to give Brady and Aspen the good news."

"I need to run by the bank, the farmers market, and the butcher. Do you want to go to the animal shelter and deliver the good news first and then return to town and catch Hap while we make the other stops?"

"Okay. Let's do that. And maybe we can grab some lunch."

"We just had breakfast."

I shrugged. "What can I say? I'm eating for two now."

Chapter 5

As predicted, Doctor Brady Baker, the local veterinarian and animal shelter owner, was thrilled and relieved to learn that Tony and I had successfully accomplished our quest of having the fireworks show moved back to its original location. I felt awful about being happy that Wilton Arlington was no longer calling the shots, given the reason for the turn of events, but I was also glad the animals wouldn't be traumatized.

"I'm not sure how you managed to do what you have, but I'm very grateful," Brady said to Tony and me. "I tried speaking to the mayor a while back, and he simply informed me that the Chamber of Commerce was paying for the event and had the right to make decisions relating to the event's location."

"I think it helped that Grandy Brown decided to move," I said.

"Grandy Brown's moving?" Brady asked.

"He is, and the mayor needed someone to take over as event chairperson for Halloween," I said.

Brady looked at Tony and smiled. "The mayor made a trade."

Tony nodded.

Brady reached out a hand and shook Tony's. "You're a good guy to take one for the team."

"Hey, I'm helping as well," I said.

Brady reached out and hugged me. Of course, once my body made contact with his body, he took a step back and looked down at my stomach.

"Do you have something to share?"

I glanced at Tony. He shrugged.

"I do, but I should speak with my mother first."

He pulled me in and hugged me again. "Understood. Congratulations to both of you."

I supposed that if Brady could figure out that I was expecting a child simply by hugging me, I really did need to bring Mom up to speed. It wasn't something I was anxious to do since I knew that once she found out about the baby, she would start smothering me with helpful advice and suggestions. But she was my mother, and I supposed that the right thing for me to do was tell her that she was going to be a grandmother again before someone else beat me to it.

After we left the animal shelter, we stopped at a lakeside deli. I had turkey on wheat, and Tony had roast beef on sourdough. The food was good, and the view was exceptional, which helped me to relax and center my emotions before heading into the second part of my day.

"So do you think I need to invite Mom to the house to tell her about the baby, or can I just pull her aside at the diner?"

"I wouldn't recommend pulling her aside at work. If you want to have more control over the situation, then my suggestion would be for us to visit her at her home and tell her then. If we invite her out to the house, it will be harder to end the visit if she isn't inclined to leave, but if we go to her, then if you start to feel overwhelmed, you merely need to say the word, and we'll make our exit."

I laughed. "It's crazy that I need a safe word when visiting my mother."

"I agree, but she has been somewhat intense as of late. To be perfectly honest, I must admit that I'm uncertain about what kind of response we should expect."

"Since Bree is pregnant as well, maybe that will dilute her focus a little," I said. "I love my mom, but she drove Bree nuts during her first pregnancy. I'm not sure if that was because Ella was her first grandchild or she was Bree's first child, so Mom felt the need to guide her through the process, but I really don't think I'm up to that much active parenting."

Tony didn't respond since we'd arrived at the parking area behind Hap's store, and he was focused on finding a parking spot large enough for his extra-long crew-cab truck, but I knew that he sympathized with my predicament, and I knew that he'd support me in whatever approach I decided worked best for me. Since Tilly was getting on in years, we no longer allowed her to jump out of the truck without aid, so when Tony opened the door and told her to wait, she patiently obeyed and waited for him to help her. The last thing we wanted was for her to suffer a shoulder or elbow injury.

"Hey, guys," Hap greeted the minute we entered the store through the back door that led out to the parking area. When Tilly and I brought the mail, we entered through the front door that opened onto the sidewalk. "Tilly, my girl, it's so good to see you."

Tilly trotted toward one of her favorite people for a hug and a treat.

"What brings you in today?"

"I need some hardware for a project, and Tess wanted to bring Tilly in for a visit," Tony answered.

"I'm so happy you did. I've been missing both my girls, but after seeing you and Tess yesterday, I realized that Tilly was the one I missed seeing the most."

"Thanks a lot," I joked good-naturedly. "I have news," I added as Tony headed off to find the supplies he'd mentioned needing.

"Oh. And what's that?"

"Tony and I got the mayor to agree to move the fireworks show back to the original location south of town."

"That is good news," Hap said. "If someone had asked me, I would have said that trying to reason with the mayor wouldn't have produced the desired outcome. What did you do to convince him?"

"It's not so much what we did as much as what we were willing to do in exchange."

Hap raised a busy white brow. "And what did you agree to do?"

"Chair the Halloween event. Apparently, Grandy Brown is moving, and the mayor desperately needed someone to step in."

Hap chuckled. "You don't say. I know that chairing the event is a huge job, but you've done it before, so I guess you know what you're getting into."

"We do. I wouldn't have volunteered under any other circumstances, but I truly wanted to get the fireworks show moved back to its original location, and agreeing to chair the Halloween event seemed to be the most expedient way of accomplishing my goal. Now, all I need to do is figure out who killed Wilton Arlington, and then I can relax and enjoy the rest of the summer."

"Still no word on that?"

I shook my head. "Not as of when I spoke to Mike last night."

"Angie was in earlier."

"Angie Gonzales?" I asked. Angie was the best electrician in town.

Hap nodded. "Angie told me that she heard from one of her customers that Wilton had been engaged in what could only be labeled as legally questionable activity before his death."

"Legally questionable activity?" I asked.

"It appears that Wilton was receiving kickbacks for pushing certain agendas through the chamber's board since becoming president. Being on the chamber's board is an unpaid position, so while some of the folks who run for the board are intent on pushing through their own agenda, most aren't passionate about the projects others bring forward and will usually go along with the majority."

"So if I want the local lodging tax to be lowered and you want free swim days at the public pool, there is a mutual understanding that I'll vote for your proposal if you vote for mine."

"Exactly, but it sounds like Wilton had been using his position as president to present and then call for a vote on several different projects without taking the time necessary to allow the board to debate the best course of action. Projects that were a bit more controversial and likely to be voted down without his interference."

"Such as?"

"Such as the new housing project near the ballfields and the out-of-state contractor hired to oversee the project, as well as the cancellation of the Fourth of July craft show in the park to make way for the carnival supported by the Rotary Club. I'm sure there may have been other projects, but those are the two Angie had heard about."

"They canceled the craft show?"

He nodded.

"I guess I hadn't heard. That must have made a lot of people mad. Most of those vendors begin making their products to sell months in advance. Why did the town allow the craft show to be canceled?"

Hap shrugged. "Angie seemed to think that Arlington had some sort of influence over the mayor and the town council. Or at least certain members of the town council. Even though the crafters have been holding their fair in the park for decades, they still needed a permit for the event, and when they applied this year, their request was denied. Angie talked to some of the crafters, and they said that the decision came down from the mayor. In the past, the mayor had always supported the event, so Angie assumed that he had been pressured to turn down the crafters in order to allow the Rotary Club to set up their carnival in that space."

"So, it's possible that someone bribed Arlington to move the fireworks show."

"Angie felt that was likely. And I have to agree. The man was adamant about moving the show. Why? Everyone was satisfied with the way things had always been, so why would he take such an unpopular stand and then hold steadfast to that stand, even when someone like you got everyone riled up and willing to protest."

Hap made a good point. Why had Arlington dug his heels in the way he had? And what did he have to gain by standing firm even in the face of opposition?

"I don't suppose Angie had any idea who might have put him up to moving the fireworks show."

Hap shook his head. "She didn't know. She said that for him to support such an unpopular decision, he was likely bribed with a huge reward or was threatened with an equally large consequence."

"So, did Angie think that it was possible he was being blackmailed?"

Hap shrugged. "She thought that might have been the case, but she made it clear that she couldn't be sure since she didn't have any evidence to substantiate her opinions."

I wasn't sure that this line of thought would lead anywhere, but the idea that Arlington had made the decisions he had for reasons other than personal preference would be interesting to explore. I'd have to mention it to Mike and see if this was an angle he'd considered. In fact, maybe we'd pop in and say hi to my favorite brother after we left here.

Once we left the hardware and home supply store, Tony wanted to grab a couple items from the farmers market, and then we headed to Mike's office.

"Tess, Tony, Tilly," Frank greeted as Tilly wandered over to say hi to Mike's dog, Leonard, who'd been napping on the dog bed near the back of the reception area of the White Eagle Police Station. "What are you all doing here today?"

"Actually, we'd like to speak to Mike. Is he in?"

"In his office. You can go on back."

I told Tilly to stay with Frank and Leonard since Mike had a small office that would be crowded enough with Mike, Tony, and me, and then we headed down the hallway.

"Hey, guys," Mike greeted us as we entered his office. "I thought I heard voices out front."

"Tony and I are in town to do errands, and we stopped in at Hap's place," I said as I sat on the chair on the far side of his desk. "Hap spoke to Angie Gonzales, and according to Hap, Angie had an interesting take on the Wilton Arlington murder. Tony and I just wanted to be sure you'd heard the same thing she'd heard."

"And what did Angie hear?"

I responded. "Angie told Hap that she'd heard that Arlington had been accepting bribes or kickbacks for pushing certain agenda items through the chamber's board."

Mike leaned back in his chair. "Really? Did she say which agenda items?"

"Hap said the housing project out near the ballfields and the out-of-state contractor hired to oversee the project, as well as the cancellation of the craft show to allow the Rotary Club to use the park on July fourth, and likely the change in venue for the fireworks show."

"Actually," Mike said, "the mayor called me, and I guess a decision has been made to move the show back to its original location."

"Did he tell you why he made that decision?" I asked.

"No, he didn't mention a reason for the change."

I proceeded to bring Mike up to speed.

"Are you sure you want to do that?" Mike said. "The Halloween event is a lot of work, and you'll be feeling the weight of your pregnancy by that point."

"If it means that the animals at the shelter won't be traumatized, then I'm sure."

Mike leaned forward, crossing his arms over each other on his desk as he did so. "So Angie thinks Arlington had been pushing specific agendas through the chamber's board over others for cash."

"Hap thought he was either being paid to push through certain proposals or was being blackmailed to do so. Hap didn't seem to know which, but he did say that Angie felt fairly certain that there was an outside influence at play."

"I suppose that either receiving bribes or acting to appease someone who had dirt on you both make good motives for murder if the deal he'd struck went bad. We pulled and reviewed Arlington's phone and financial records, but nothing popped." Mike looked at Tony. "Maybe you could do a deeper dive."

"I can do that. It would help to know what you already have so I can figure out the best starting point," Tony said to Mike.

"I'll email you the file. I'd say we could look around in Arlington's home office, but his home office no longer exists. Any evidence that might have been found within the structure is long gone."

"We drove past the place," I said. "Talk about total destruction. All that's left is ash."

"The fire was incredibly intense," Mike added. "If not for the fact that Arlington lived on a large piece of property and there weren't any other houses for at least an eighth of a mile in any direction, the fire would likely have taken out an entire neighborhood."

"Any idea why Arlington had the fireworks in his home rather than a storage facility or warehouse?" Tony asked.

"It was determined that the fireworks had been stored in a shed attached to the house but accessed from outside. While it originally appeared that fireworks had been inside the house, when the fire inspector did his thing, he was able to trace the explosion to its source."

"I understand that a fuse was used to ignite the fire," I said.

"That's correct," Mike confirmed. "The fuse at the point of ignition was turned to ash like everything else, but there was a piece of the fuse found in the forest which seemed to line up perfectly with the shed the fireworks had been stored in.

"I know that Arlington couldn't have known that someone would light the dang things on fire, but it still seems pretty irresponsible to have that much firepower anywhere near your home," I said.

Mike agreed. He also stated that without input from Arlington, which obviously wasn't possible, there didn't appear to be any way to determine why the man had made the decisions he had.

"I know that I said I'd stay out of things, but you must realize that I'm anxious about getting this whole thing wrapped up so I can get on with my life," I said to Mike.

"I understand."

"I don't suppose you have an update you wouldn't mind sharing."

He hesitated but then began to speak. "If I keep you in the loop, do you swear that you will not investigate on your own without Tony or me being right there with you?"

"I promise."

"I need to be sure. I don't want anything bad to happen to my unborn niece or nephew."

"What about your sister?" I asked.

He smiled. "I don't want anything to happen to my sister either. Swear to me."

"I swear. Now, what do you know?"

"As you know, Arlington's body was burned to the point where it was impossible to make a statement about the cause of death. We're assuming that the cause of death was the fire, but it is possible that someone could have shot, stabbed, or strangled him first and then set the fire to hide the evidence."

"Yes, I had heard that there was a rumor about the actual cause of death making the rounds," I said. "I also heard that you have evidence that the man was involved in an altercation before the fire."

Mike nodded. "We have a witness who saw a dark blue sedan parked in front of Arlington's home shortly before the fire. He thought it might have been a BMW, but he wasn't a hundred percent positive. The witness stated that he hadn't noticed the car's driver or thought to get a license plate number since nothing had happened at the time of the sighting. The witness did notice that the car was parked oddly on the driveway, almost as if the driver had sped up but stopped with no regard for the designated parking area. He also said that he heard shouting coming from inside the home. I guess the windows were open, and the sound of the voices carried all the way out to the street where he was walking his dog."

"So Arlington argued with someone before the explosion," I stated.

Mike nodded again. "A female someone. The man, who had been passing by, lives in the next house over from Arlington's property. He shared that he was new to the neighborhood and didn't know Arlington well, but the man also said that he'd noticed a lot of different vehicles coming and going from Arlington's home. The man told me that the only reason he stopped to take note of the sedan was because of the haphazard way it was parked and, of course, the sound of an argument coming from inside the house. When the house literally blew up half an hour after the neighbor returned from his walk, he called the station and talked to Frank. Frank canvassed the neighborhood, hoping to find someone who might have seen the sedan, but, at the time, no one he spoke to admitted to having seen it. Then, this morning, one of Arlington's neighbors contacted Frank. The neighbor, Dave, who didn't provide a last name, shared that he'd been out of town when the police came around but indicated that he remembered seeing the car the day he left town. He confirmed that the sedan was a BMW and thought it was an Eight Series. He told Frank that he didn't write the license plate number down, but he did recognize the plates as being issued in Nevada."

"I guess that does narrow it down a bit, but not a lot," I said.

"It's a start," Mike said.

It was a start. Since it seemed that Mike had everything covered, there wasn't anything for me to do other than go home and take a nap. I can't even begin to tell you how frustrated and useless that made me feel.

Chapter 6

By the time Kiwi and I woke up from our nap, I could hear Tony doing something outside on the patio. Tilly had been sleeping on the bed next to me, but the cats and the other dogs were nowhere to be found. I supposed the dogs at least were outside with Tony. Motioning for Tilly to follow, I grabbed my shoes and headed downstairs.

"Wow, look how much you got done," I said as I stepped outside into the warm sunshine. "I thought you were going to do some digging for Mike."

"I did. You took a long nap."

"What time is it?"

"After four."

I guess I had taken a long nap.

"Have a seat on the lounge chair, and I'll grab us something to drink," Tony suggested.

"I can grab the drinks," I said. "You have dirt on your hands already, so you may as well finish up. Did you find anything during your research?"

Tony nodded as he grabbed his hand trowel and began to dig a small hole for the next flower. "I did find a few oddities. I called and spoke to Mike, and he plans to follow up. It's likely that he'll need additional information once he speaks to a few people, but it didn't make sense to continue with my search until he got the answers needed to make sense of what I found, so I decided to work out here."

"And what exactly did you find?"

Tony paused. He straightened and looked in my direction. "Why don't you grab those drinks while I wash up, and then we can talk."

I would have preferred to have my curiosity assuaged immediately, but I agreed to Tony's plan. There was a pitcher of freshly squeezed lemonade Tony must have made while I was napping, so I filled two glasses with ice, grabbed the pitcher and glasses, and headed back to the patio. Once Tony finished washing up, he joined me.

"So?" I asked, almost before he could sit down.

"I found a text on Arlington's phone instructing a man named Bodine Cosgrove to call him on his other phone. He provided a phone number, which allowed me to trace the phone to a business. The business the second phone was registered to seems to be a dummy corporation, but I did manage to obtain a small amount of information, such as the company's name and the names of the stockholders and the board of directors."

"Okay, so what's the name of this dummy company?"

"Idlewild Development. Idlewild Development only has three stockholders, Wilton Arlington, Bruce Arlington, and Ronald Arlington. Ronald Arlington is Wilton's uncle. I tracked the man down, and he's currently a resident in a memory care facility. He's been there for a couple of years, so it's unlikely that he is an active member of Idlewild Development. Ronald is listed as a board member, but I spoke to his doctor, who assured me that Ronald was well past the point where he would be able to understand anything he might be asked to vote on."

"And what about Bruce?" I asked.

"Bruce Arlington was Wilton's brother. He died in an auto accident about a year ago. I don't have all the details at this point since Mike offered to follow up on things after I spoke to him, so I didn't dig deeper, but based on the day of incorporation for Idlewild Development and the date of the obituary that I found for Bruce Arlington, it appears that the man died just two months after the company was established."

Okay. This whole thing sounded fishy, but I wasn't sure what it meant.

"So, other than Idlewild Development's existence, did you discover anything else about the company?" I asked.

"As far as I can tell, even though Idlewild Development has never developed anything, there have been a series of deposits, which total over a hundred thousand dollars, made into the company's bank account. If I had to guess, I'd say that if Wilton Arlington had been accepting bribes or kickbacks in exchange for votes, he was using the company to launder the cash."

"Can you follow the deposits and see if you can figure this all out?"

"I can, but when I spoke to Mike, he told me he planned to follow up. This is his case. He is the cop. My plan at this point is to wait and see what Mike wants me to do next. In the meantime, I plan to play around in my garden, spend quality time with my wife, and start planning the nursery I suddenly feel an overwhelming urge to get started on."

To an extent, I supposed Tony's plan made sense, but I was at the point where I was beyond being content to sit around and do nothing when there was obviously work still needing to be done. "Maybe I'll call and talk to Mike," I suggested.

"I just spoke to him an hour ago," Tony reminded me. "He'll need time to track down the leads I provided him. Maybe we should go and talk to your mother. You seem antsy to get out and do something, and sharing our good news with your mother is something that really does need to be addressed sooner rather than later now that others are beginning to find out about Kiwi's existence."

"The diner's still open, and we agreed to talk to her at home."

"The diner closes in less than two hours. By the time I clean up and we drive into town, your mom will just be getting home," Tony pointed out. "Look, I know that you are concerned that your mom is going to smother you with helpful advice once she finds out about the baby, but we still need to tell her. I really do think it's time."

"Okay," I agreed. "I'll call Mom to make sure she's planning to head home after work. I'll tell her that we planned on being in town anyway, and we wanted to check in with her about some of the plans for the party. If she's going to be home, we'll stop by."

Tony leaned forward and kissed me on the forehead. "I'll clean things up out here and then hit the shower."

Tony tried to take my mind off things as we drove toward White Eagle. I knew I should be excited to share my news with the people in my life who I loved the most, but so far, the whole thing had seemed overwhelming. It wasn't as if my pregnancy had come from out of nowhere. Tony and I had decided to start trying this past February while we were vacationing in Tahoe. The fact that I conceived right away was a bit of a surprise since I'd really thought it would take at least several months, but we were ready, and I knew I should be happy rather than scared.

Tony reminded me that my mom was going to be thrilled for me. He reminded me that she'd been going through something as of late and that bringing her good news was something that we should both be happy about doing. I knew he was right, but I still couldn't help but feel butterflies in the pit of my stomach.

"Tess, Tony. I'm so glad you decided to stop by. Even though I've spoken to you both on the phone about the party, I've barely seen you since you returned from Ashton Falls."

"We've been pretty busy," I said as Mom escorted us through the house and onto the back patio, where she'd set out a bottle of wine and three glasses.

"Once of my customers at the diner gave me this bottle of wine from his vineyard in Napa. I've been waiting to have someone come by so I could share it."

I placed a hand on Mom's arm. "Actually, I'm going to pass."

She looked me in the eye. "Are you ill?"

"No. Not ill." I took her hand in mine. "But I am expecting."

There. I'd said it. I was glad I got it out of the way right away.

"Expecting!" Mom reached forward and hugged me hard. She then pulled back and ran a hand over my stomach. "How far along are you?"

"Four months. And before you comment about waiting so long to fill everyone in, I found out while we were out of town and just needed to take some time to get used to the idea before I brought anyone else in on things."

I half expected Mom to be mad, but she didn't seem mad. Instead of going crazy and starting to dole out advice or immediately overwhelming me with plans, Mom took my hand in hers and suggested that I sit down. She then instructed Tony to go inside and find something non-alcoholic for us all to share. After Tony left, she sat down at the outdoor table where she'd planned to serve the wine and very calmly asked me how I'd been doing with the whole thing.

"It's taken me some time to get used to the idea, but I'm fine," I answered.

"Any morning sickness?"

"Not much. A few bouts here and there, but nothing like what Bree experienced."

"Poor Bree has had a tough time with both pregnancies, but this one has gone smoother than the first. I've always thought you'd do better with all the physical and emotional changes. You've always been the resilient sort." She put her hand over mine and gave it a squeeze. "Knowing you, you likely don't need anything from your mama, but if you do need something, you know I'm here for you. All you need to do is ask."

I smiled. "I know, Mom. And I appreciate that. Tony has been taking good care of me, and I have been fine, really."

Tony came out with iced peach tea. He assured me that it was herbal and contained no caffeine. Mom thanked him for the tea and congratulated him on his status of expectant father while I sat and wondered who the woman calmly hugging her son-in-law was and where the woman I was convinced would go crazy with baby plans had gone.

Mom asked a few questions about my due date and whether or not I knew the baby's gender. I shared that I was due in December and that I planned to have an ultrasound to find out the gender during my doctor's appointment later this week. She asked if we'd settled on names, and I told her we hadn't. She then completely dropped the subject of grandchild number three to ask about the food for the Fourth of July party and whether I thought it might be a good idea to drop the plan to grill chicken and ribs and simply bring in deli sandwiches and deli-made salads.

"I don't mind manning the grill," Tony said. "And I think Tess and I are up to throwing a few salads together."

"Whatever you think is best, dear. I just want to be sure that we don't go overboard. Both my girls will need to take it easy, and this is just a party. Nothing important enough to cause either Bree or Tess any sort of stress."

I had the strongest urge to pinch myself since I was sure this must be a dream, but the overly hyper mom I'd been dealing with for months now seemed to have reverted back to her pre-manic self.

She looked at Tony. "If you can take care of the chicken and ribs, that would be great, and if you have time, I've been craving your famous pasta salad. Sam's friend, Gus, offered to bring potato salad, which I've been assured will be the best I've ever tasted, and Sam and I will take care of the appetizers. Hattie is going to provide the dessert, and Aunt Ruthie is going to bring her baked beans as well as sourdough loaves for grilling. I told Bree that if she wanted to bring something and felt up to it, we would happily include it, but if she wasn't up to cooking, we'd have plenty without it."

"Gus?" I asked.

"He's an old friend of Sam's," Mom explained. "I'm not really sure how they met, but he's in town and plans to stay for a while, so Sam invited him to the party."

I glanced at Tony. He shrugged. If Gus was an old friend of Sam's, then it was at least possible that he was an old friend of Dad's. I supposed it might be a good idea to ask Mike if Dad had mentioned him during their early morning breakfasts.

Tony and I chatted with Mom for another hour before she announced that Sam would be stopping by soon and that she needed to get ready. She suggested that I call her after my ultrasound, which I agreed to do, and then she hugged us both and showed us to the door.

"Okay, that was weird, right?" I asked Tony when we made it back to his truck.

"Your mother was much calmer about the news that grandbaby number three was on the way than either of us expected," Tony admitted.

"It's not that I'm not happy with the way our talk went, but I have to admit that I kept waiting for the other shoe to drop the whole time we were with her."

Tony started the engine and pulled away from the curb. "Your mom wasn't overly intense when I met her. In fact, she was the opposite of intense. I realize that her behavior over the past couple of years seems to have changed, but perhaps she was dealing with a hormonal unbalance that has righted itself. She is at that age."

"I guess."

"So, do you feel better?" Tony asked.

I smiled. "I do. Now that Mike, Bree, and Mom know about Kiwi, I don't have to worry about the secret getting out. I guess we can start telling our friends as it seems appropriate. Brady knows, but I'd like to tell Aspen. And Hap and Hattie. There are only a few people I want to talk to before they find out from someone else, so maybe we can make a trip into town tomorrow."

Tony opened his mouth to respond when his cell phone rang. He answered it with his Bluetooth. "Hey, Mike. You have Tess and Tony on speaker. We're driving home from a visit with your mom."

"Did you share your news?"

"We did," I answered.

"And?"

"And she was happy but calm. She wasn't overly hyper about it at all. It was actually somewhat odd."

"Bree dropped by the diner today to show Mom the invitations she wants to use for the baby shower Mom and Aunt Ruthie are planning to throw for her in August, and she said the same thing about Mom's overall mood and anxiety level. She said that she seemed like her old self. Calm and almost detached. She was worried that something was wrong with her, but then she decided to simply enjoy the change and try not to overthink things."

"It does seem that whatever had been driving her anxiety has resolved itself. The manic tension I've come to associate with her has completely dissipated," I agreed. "I can see why Bree might be worried, but I, for one, am going to simply embrace the change."

"Agreed."

"I'm assuming you called to talk to Tony about the case. We're only a few miles out of town. We can turn around and stop by if that would be easier."

"Actually, that might be better if you're up for it," Mike agreed.

I assured him that we'd be at his house in about fifteen minutes, and then Tony executed a U-turn and headed in that direction.

Chapter 7

When we arrived at Mike and Bree's home, we found Bree in her pajamas and curled up with a fluffy blanket in the recliner. Since it was a warm evening, Mike had even turned the air conditioner on so Bree wouldn't get hot while she snuggled. Ella had already been put to bed, and it seemed clear that Mike had been sitting on the sofa watching a movie, so Tony and I joined them in the living room.

"Thanks for coming back to town," Mike said. "We could have gone over this on the phone, but it will be easier to discuss face to face."

"No problem," Tony said. "What did you find out?"

Mike crossed one leg over the other and began to speak. "I used the information we found related to the blue sedan the witness saw parked in front of Arlington's home shortly before the fire and tracked it to a woman named Gloria Arlington."

"A sister?" I asked, picking up on the fact she shared a last name with the victim.

"Sister-in-law," Mike corrected. "Gloria, who lives in Nevada, apparently left White Eagle the day after the explosion. Since I couldn't personally interview her, I called a buddy of mine, Chris Tomassini. Chris is a cop who happens to live and work in Nevada. He agreed to speak to her on my behalf, and according to Chris, Gloria had been married to Bruce Arlington before his death."

"One of the three stockholders listed in the documents for the dummy corporation Tony found," I said.

"Exactly. Apparently, Bruce left a real mess in terms of his finances when he passed, which Gloria has been trying to unravel ever since her husband's accident. After coming to the realization that her husband had bank accounts and investments that she didn't even know about, she hired a private investigator to help her make sense of the mess she'd been left with when her husband passed. I guess it was the PI who found Idlewild Developers. The PI told Gloria that the company seemed to have a lot of cash assets, and as can be expected in situations such as this, Gloria was interested in getting her hands on her husband's share of that cash. According to Chris, Gloria indicated that she called and spoke to Wilton, who told her that Bruce's shares reverted to him with his death. Gloria was unwilling to accept that, so she asked her PI to do some additional digging. According to the PI, Gloria should have been the one to inherit the stock. She decided to come to White Eagle and talk to Wilton about it face to face, which was the arguing the neighbor heard, but she swears she didn't kill him."

"Do you believe her?" I asked.

Mike hesitated and then answered. "I'm not sure. Chris told me that she appeared to be telling the truth when he spoke to her, but I did some additional digging into the corporation, and it seems that Wilton, who wasn't married, actually named Bruce as his beneficiary in the event of his death. Of course, Bruce preceded Wilton in death, so it's unclear if Bruce's beneficiary, Gloria, would have a claim to Wilton's assets or if a next of kin will be sought out, but it does seem there might be something going on there. I also question the timing of Gloria's visit with the explosion. Her husband died a year ago, and on the exact day she decides to come to White Eagle to confront Wilton, he dies?"

"That does seem unlikely," I said.

Mike looked at Tony. "The reason for my call was to ask if you would be willing to dig even deeper into Idlewild Development and the wills both Bruce and Wilton left behind. It would be interesting to know how Gloria might play in the entire picture."

"You think she knows more than she said, and her endgame was to cash in," Tony confirmed.

"I suspect that could be the case."

Tony shrugged. "I have time. I'll see what I can find. Tess and I plan to come into town tomorrow to share our news about the baby with a handful of people whom Tess wants to personally tell before the word spreads, but I'll fit your search in."

"I'm so happy that your mom took the news so calmly," Bree said. "I could tell you were really stressing over that."

I frowned. "You didn't happen to talk to Mom beforehand, did you?"

"What? No way. I would never share your secret."

Her words indicated that she hadn't talked to Mom, but her expression suggested otherwise. Bree might be telling the truth, but if I knew Bree, and I did, she'd been afraid that Mom would go crazy the way she had when Bree had announced her pregnancy with Ella, so she'd been proactive and talked it through with her before I'd had the chance to speak to her. On the one hand, I supposed I should be annoyed with this, but on the other hand, I was happy that things worked out the way they had, so maybe my best move would be to just let it go. The reality was that now that everyone who truly mattered knew, I could relax and enjoy the experience.

I looked at Mike. "If you're done with Tony, I want to ask about Sam's friend, Gus. Mom mentioned the name when we were talking about the upcoming party. Do you happen to know anything about him?"

"No. Should I?"

"Maybe not. Mom just said that Gus was an old friend of Sam's who they invited to the party, and I figured that if Gus was an old friend of Sam's, then he may have been an old friend of Dad's. Since you've been talking to Dad, I thought he might have mentioned him since it sounds like he's been in town for a while."

"Dad hasn't mentioned him," Mike said. "But I'm sure Sam has old friends who aren't in any way related to Dad or the black ops group they both worked for. Childhood friends, for example, or friends of the family."

"Family? What family? Sam is as secretive about his past as Dad has been."

Mike nodded. "I guess that's true, but that doesn't mean that both Sam and Dad don't have people from their past that they try to stay in touch with."

I supposed Mike had a point, but I guessed that I just assumed since our dad never talked about anyone from his past, that meant he didn't have anyone to talk about.

"You said that you and Dad have been talking about random things," I said. "Has he ever mentioned anything that might give us a glimpse into his childhood? I know what he told us about his childhood when we were kids, which wasn't a lot, but we must have someone. Uncles, aunts, or cousins."

Mike shrugged. "He's never said one way or the other. He might talk about baseball, but he's never shared personal stories, such as attending a game with a parent or grandparent when he was a kid. I remember the guy at the lake where Mom wanted to go for Thanksgiving that year knew a few things about his past, so it isn't like he was just dropped out of the sky onto the earth as a fully grown spy on the run. If Dad and I can continue the relationship we're just getting started with, maybe I can ask him to fill in some of the blanks."

As dangerous as I thought Mike's relationship with Dad was, the reality was that I'd cherish the chance to learn even a little about the man whom I called Dad but didn't really know.

"When I was a kid, I remember Dad telling me about some of the camping trips he went on," Mike said. "I guess I was maybe ten at the time. I was supposed to go camping with my Boy Scout troop, but I'd come down with the flu and had to stay home. Dad was between runs and happened to be home at the time, and he came into my room and tried to cheer me up. By the time I was ten, Dad was gone most of the time and withdrawn when he was home, and I remember being surprised since he seemed to be in a good mood on this particular day."

"Do you remember what he told you?" I asked.

"He made a comment about how everything was too organized these days. He was talking about the very structured camping trip the Scouts were going on since earning badges was the objective of the camping trip. I don't remember everything he said, but Dad shared details about a few camping trips he went on as a kid. It seems that Dad and his buddies would take off for a long weekend with only a fishing pole, a sleeping bag, and a few random supplies such as matches and dry socks. He assured me that I wasn't missing out on anything by not being able to attend the campout that weekend with the Scouts. He told me how it felt to be in the woods with just a few supplies and a handful of friends. He also told me that once I was feeling better, he and I would take a real camping trip, just us guys."

"And did he ever take you?"

"No, but I guess I never expected that he would. I knew Dad well enough to know that while he was trying to cheer me up by telling me the two of us would go camping, I also knew him well enough to know we never would."

I wasn't sure if the story was sweet or sad. It was sweet of Dad to do what he had done to cheer Mike up after he missed his camping trip. But even though Mike said that he hadn't expected Dad to follow through with the father/son camping trip, if I knew Mike, and I did, that was exactly what he expected, and knowing Mike, it must have hurt him deeply when Dad didn't follow through.

"Would either of you like some coffee or something else to drink?" Bree asked.

Tony and I assured her we were good and couldn't stay long.

"Do you think it might be worthwhile to review the chamber's minutes for the past year or two to see if we can identify which transactions Wilton Arlington may have pushed through?" I asked. "I'm thinking about transactions that appear to be suspicious, like the housing project. Not only is the land where the project is being built considered sensitive, but it's customary to hire local contractors. If local contractors weren't even considered and the out-of-state contractor, who was awarded the contract, was simply handed the job, that would be odd."

"That's true, but isn't that a town thing and not a Chamber of Commerce thing?" Bree asked. "Based on what I understand, the town council approved the project and agreed to the out-of-state contractor, not the chamber."

"That's true," I said. "But the theory I've been working with is that not only was Arlington somehow benefiting from these transactions, but he had something on the mayor he was using to get him to go along with his plots."

"Tess does have a point," Mike said. "It may have been the town council and the town planner who approved both the project and the contractor, but I did have Frank dig around a bit, and it does appear that Arlington was the one who was pushing the whole thing from the beginning."

"So maybe I need to do some digging into the mayor's finances," Tony said. "Of course, even if I'm careful, there is a certain risk anytime I use my hacking skills to gain sensitive information, so before I do anything, I guess we need to be sure that digging into the mayor is really that important."

"Unless we consider him a suspect in Arlington's murder, I guess it might not be," I said. I looked at Mike. "Is he?"

"Not at this point, but I will admit that he seems to have been more involved than I initially thought. Not just with the housing project but with the fireworks show as well. I mean, it might have been Arlington who wanted to move the show, but the town denied a permit for the old location and approved one for the new location."

"Yeah, and after Tony and I negotiated with the mayor, he managed to move the fireworks show back to the original location within the hour, which seems to indicate that he had the power to approve any site he might decide on," I added.

"Maybe I should take a closer look at those junctures where the activities being sponsored by the chamber and the need for town approval intersect," Mike concluded. "If the two were colluding, then a pattern should emerge."

Since Bree looked exhausted, I suggested that we should head home. Tony agreed. He also agreed to do additional research and check in with Mike the following day. Even though I had promised to stay home and not head out sleuthing as I usually would have done, I still felt I had a vested interest in having this investigation put to bed, so if I thought of something I could do to help, I'd likely try to do it.

Chapter 8

Tony and I headed toward town the following morning. I had the feeling that now that the cat was out of the bag regarding my prenatal state, word would get out, and I really did have a handful of people I wanted to tell myself. Our first stop was the animal shelter, where Aspen, who hadn't been there when Tony and I had stopped by yesterday to give Brady the great news about the fireworks show, ran up and hugged me.

"Thank you, thank you, thank you."

I knew she was referring to the fact that Tony and I had managed to avoid a near catastrophe should the fireworks show have been held near the animal shelter as had been the plan.

"Anything for the animals," I said, hugging her tightly.

She must have felt the bump since she stepped back and looked at my stomach.

"Yes," I said. "Tony and I are expecting, which is why we're here. We wanted to tell you personally before someone else spilled the beans."

"Oh my gosh, Tess!" She hugged me again. "I'm so happy for you." She glanced at Tony. "Both of you. When did you find out?"

"While we were in Ashton Falls, actually. I know we've been back for a few weeks, and I could have mentioned it at any point, but I wanted to tell my mother first, which I procrastinated doing. We finally told her last night, so here we are telling you."

"I'm honored and thrilled to be one of your first. Does Zoe know?"

"She does. She was there when we found out. I asked her not to say anything, and she promised not to."

"Wow." She hugged her arms around her waist. "I'm so excited. When are you due?"

"December."

"A Christmas baby. You must be so excited."

I glanced at Tony and smiled. "We really are."

"Do you know if you're having a boy or a girl?"

"Not yet. I have a doctor's appointment tomorrow. We plan to find out then."

Tony and I chatted with Aspen for a few more minutes, and then we headed toward the hardware and home supply store to talk to Hap. We figured we'd share our news with him and then head directly to Hattie's bakeshop to fill her in before anyone beat us to it. As expected, both Hap and Hattie were thrilled with our news, and as expected, both wanted to be kept in the loop with respect to the gender reveal. Hattie asked if we planned to have a party to reveal the gender of our child to our friends and family, to which we replied that, given the party we were hosting on July fourth, we didn't want to plan an additional party. But I promised that we would be sure to stop by and let her know how our doctor's appointment went once we told Mom and Bree, who would disown us if we didn't tell them first.

"Lunch?" Tony asked after we'd spoken to those we felt we needed to share our secret with.

"Lunch sounds good, and even though I'm not usually a huge fan of fried pickles, I've been craving them all day for some reason."

"The café on the lake not only has good fried pickles but outdoor seating as well." Tony looked up toward the deep blue sky. "It is a really nice day."

"Actually, that sounds good. The café has a good Cobb salad, although I wouldn't mind having French fries."

"So get a salad with a side of fries. We'll have the fried pickles as an appetizer."

During the first trimester of my pregnancy, I hadn't really had any odd cravings, but now that I'd entered my second trimester, I found that I was eating like a trucker. I guessed it was a good thing I was naturally thin. Of course, having worked as a mail carrier for so many years, walking miles upon miles most days was also a factor in my being thin. Now that I was retired, I supposed I'd need to watch what I ate. Starting tomorrow. Today was going to be all about fried pickles, Cobb salad with extra bacon, and hot and salty French fries.

When we arrived at the café, we found that our favorite table on the deck near the water was open, so I hurried to snag the table while Tony went to the front to let the hostess know that we were there and that we'd seated ourselves. Technically, we probably should have waited to be seated, but this was a casual place where seating yourself wasn't usually frowned upon, and I didn't want to risk losing the table to someone who might have shown up behind us.

Tony met me at the table with two glasses of water.

"We're all set," he said. "I went ahead and placed our order."

"Fried pickles with ranch?"

"Yes."

"Cobb salad, extra bacon, extra cheese?"

He nodded.

"French fries with ranch, ketchup, and hot mustard on the side?"

"I didn't order the hot mustard, but yes to the rest."

I opened my mouth to complain about the mustard, but then he reminded me of the horrific heartburn I'd had the last time I'd eaten the hot mustard and I decided to let it drop.

"Do you see the two women at the table by the umbrella?" I whispered.

Tony looked in that direction. "Tina Fathum and Holly Jones."

Tina was the vice president of the Chamber of Commerce, which I supposed with Arlington's death meant that she was now acting president. Holly was a chamber employee who paid bills, took care of the books, and provided other administrative support.

"Unfortunately, the women are speaking softly, so I haven't been able to pick up everything they are saying, but the word *irregularities* has been tossed around more than once during the course of their conversation," I said in my quietest voice.

"I suppose there would be irregularities to discover if Arlington had been manipulating the chamber's vote," Tony said.

"I still can't decide if the guy was taking bribes or kickbacks to pad his personal bank account or if he was being blackmailed into doing what he did. I think that knowing that will matter when it comes to trying to link his activities with a motive for his murder."

"I agree," Tony said. "When we get home, I'll head down to the computer room and see what I can find out while you take your afternoon nap."

I'd never been much of a nap person and didn't want to start being one now, but Tony realized that after about half a day, Kiwi and I needed to refuel and recharge and encouraged me to indulge in a nap each afternoon.

"If the deposits into Idlewild Developments track back to votes, then I suppose we can assume that it was bribes rather than blackmail that motivated Arlington to do what he did," I said as I continued trying to work the whole thing out in my mind. "The thing I don't understand is why. The guy seemed to do okay as a real estate agent. I'm not saying he would be considered rich, but he had a nice home on a large piece of property, and he's driven a nice car since I've known him. He wasn't married, and as far as I know, he didn't have children, so he likely didn't have hidden expenses related to family members. Why would a guy who was a member of a tight-knit community risk it all for a few bucks if he didn't really need those few bucks?"

"Good question. If I dig deep enough, I suppose I might be able to find the source of the financial bleed because it does seem likely there must have been one."

The waitress brought the fried pickles to our table and asked if we wanted anything to drink other than the water Tony had brought out.

"I'll take lemonade," I said.

Tony made a face. "Lemonade with fried pickles and ranch dressing?"

I shrugged. "It sounds good."

Tony told the waitress he'd stick with water before she hurried off to grab my lemonade.

"Don't turn around, but Jason Willis is walking up the walkway in this direction," I said. Jason was another Chamber of Commerce board member. In addition to Arlington, who had been president of the chamber before his death, Tina had been the vice president, and Jason had been on the board, along with three other men and other women. I wasn't surprised when Jason walked past our table and joined Tina and Holly at their table. He sat down and raised a hand to motion for the server to bring him a menu. Once he'd placed his order, he turned his attention to the women he'd obviously come to meet.

"I guess those left on the board must have a bit of a mess to deal with," I said. "Even if Arlington had been running things on the up and up, the sudden death of the chamber's president is bound to create at least a bit of havoc. If Arlington was involved in things only he knew about, then the remaining members would likely have a real problem."

"Holly just handed Jason a large manilla envelope," Tony said.

Since Tony was facing the table and I had my back to the group, receiving the update was appreciated.

"Did he open it? Can you tell what's in it?"

"Documents of some sort. Jason pulled them out, took a quick look, and then put them back. He set the envelope on the table and then placed his car keys on it."

"He must want to make sure he doesn't forget the envelope. When I'm out and about, I always put my keys, purse, or something important near anything I don't want to forget to take with me."

"Jason pulled his cell phone out and made a call," Tony said. "It looks like he just left a message since he only said a few words and then hung up. Maybe Mike should simply ask someone on the chamber's board what was going on with Arlington and the suspicious activity that seems to have accompanied him as the chamber's elected president. Just because we suspect Arlington of shady transactions doesn't mean the entire board is shady. Gigi Wilson has been on the board for at least a decade. I've always thought that she seemed to be the sort who did what she did because she really loves this town. If something shady was occurring, chances are that Gigi wasn't aware of it, but if she did have suspicions, I bet she'd share them."

"Gigi can be trusted," I agreed, "but I believe things will probably go better if we stop by and chat with her. She's still mad at Mike for issuing her a ticket when, after multiple warnings, she refused to keep her dog inside despite the fact that he wouldn't stop barking at the kids who live next door, but she seems to have a little crush on you."

"Gigi is seventy-eight," Tony pointed out.

"She is, but she still recognizes a hot guy when she sees one."

Tony smiled and agreed that we could pay Gigi a very short visit after we ate, but then we were absolutely going home so that I didn't become overly tired.

As I predicted she would be, Gigi was thrilled when Tony knocked on her door. She graciously invited us both inside, but I could see that Tony was the one who held her attention.

"Now, to what do I owe the pleasure of your visit?" she asked, directing her question to Tony once she'd offered us a seat on her sofa.

"I guess you heard about Wilton Arlington," Tony said.

"I did." She shook her head. "What a way to go. At least, it appears he went quickly."

"That does appear to be the case," I agreed.

"The reason we're here is to ask about some of the decisions the Chamber of Commerce has made over the past few months," Tony said. "During the investigation, we've found a few oddities that we felt warranted more of an explanation, and we figured that as a long-standing member of the board, you'd be in a position to know if there was anything irregular going on."

She responded. "Arlington tended to go his own way. Not that he could do much of anything without board support and approval, but he had this way of wrapping every little initiative up in so much paperwork that most of the members on the board simply wouldn't take the time to read through everything. It was easier for most to do what Wilton counseled them to do. Not me, mind you. I read every word of every report and voted consciously. The problem I would encounter on those occasions when I disagreed with Wilton was that I was outvoted."

"Were there others who dared to vote against Wilton's recommendations?" Tony asked.

"Tina Fathum tended to take the time to read what was presented. There are, or at least were, nine members on the board, including Arlington. As president, Arlington only voted in the event of a tie. If there was a split decision, most of the time, it would be me, Tina, and maybe one other member voting against Arlington's recommendation while the other five voted in favor. In the rare instances when we were split four to four, Arlington would vote how he wanted, so he basically won every time."

"Do you believe that Arlington was involved in something shady?" I asked.

Gigi glanced at me but then returned her attention to Tony. "I think he was, but I could never prove anything. I tried talking to the others, but Tina was the only one who would give me the time of day. If truth be told, I don't think the others wanted to risk getting on the man's wrong side. He seemed the sort to find a way to remove those who got in his way, if you know what I mean."

Actually, I did know what she meant. Tony thanked Gigi for taking the time to speak to us, and then we headed home. I was ready for a short nap, and Tony had a few ideas he wanted to track down, so he informed me that he'd be downstairs in the computer room and that I should just come down and get him when I woke up. I hadn't planned to sleep more than thirty minutes, so when I woke to find that two hours had passed, I realized I must have been more tired than I thought.

"I'm sorry I slept so long," I said, still feeling somewhat groggy as I joined him in the computer room.

"You've had a tough few days. I suspect that you and Kiwi both needed to refuel and recharge."

"Did you find anything?" I asked as I sat down on the chair next to his.

"Actually, I found a few things."

"Such as?"

Tony leaned back in his chair. He turned a little bit so that he was partially facing me. "I was curious, as you have been, about why Arlington was so adamant about moving the fireworks show from the location where it has always been to the lake near the animal shelter. Not only was the move controversial, but I couldn't see how making the move would benefit anyone. Even if he had been taking bribes for pushing certain proposals through the chamber's board voting process, why would anyone care enough about moving the show to deal with all the controversy?"

"The why of the whole thing has been on my mind as well," I said. "The pushback from animal-loving members of the community has been fierce. The fact that Arlington was sticking to his guns when I couldn't see any logical reason for him to have done so was crazy. Did you find anything?"

"Maybe. I'm still trying to sort the whole thing out. I did some research, and it appears that Jacob Everson of Everson Development purchased a hundred acres of land, including the meadow and the lake where Arlington wanted the fireworks show moved to, back in December of two thousand nineteen, just before the pandemic. The land was previously public land managed by the Bureau of Land Management, but it seems like Everson approached the BLM about buying the land with the idea of eventually developing the property. The land, as you know, is located in close proximity to other developed land, so after a bit of back and forth, the sale of the land was approved."

Being the sort who really enjoyed our undeveloped land, I wasn't thrilled with the idea, but White Eagle had been undergoing a population explosion in the past few years, and I supposed that the new residents moving to the area needed somewhere to live and places to shop.

"What does a proposed development have to do with the Fourth of July fireworks?" I asked.

"That's a good question. Apparently, there's a clause in the contract between the BLM and Everson Development that outlines a few extremely well-defined conditions under which the sale of the property can be unwound and the land returned to protected status. One of the conditions mentioned in the contract addresses the discovery of an endangered species living on the property. This condition is in effect right up until the day the land is developed. I found an email in Arlington's saved file from Everson, who had been contacted by a wildlife attorney, notifying him that two hikers had spotted a Black Footed Ferret on the property. The Black Footed Ferret is the most endangered mammal in Montana and, therefore, is protected. Proof that this specific ferret had made its home on the property would trigger the buyback clause. The attorney asked Everson to pause any plans for development until the claim made by the hikers could be verified one way or the other. In the email from Everson to Arlington, Everson outlined the situation and then asked for Arlington's help. He made mention of an arrangement between the men, but he didn't go into any specifics about the arrangement. I did some digging, and it looks as if Arlington is listed as a partner on the incorporation paperwork for Everson Development. I'm still looking into it, but it appears that Arlington had a financial stake in the company while Everson is considered to be the managing partner."

"So if the contract between Everson Development and the BLM was reversed, both Everson and Arlington stood to lose whatever profit they planned to make from the project they would eventually develop," I confirmed.

"Exactly. I've contacted Mike, and he plans to look into it, but if I had to guess, when Everson asked Arlington for help with the ferret problem, Arlington came back with the idea of a big noisy fireworks show, accompanied by a big noisy crowd to send the ferret scurrying for a new home. Of course, I have no way to prove what Arlington's thought process might have been when he decided to move the event, but the explanation I came up with makes sense."

Tony's explanation made sense to me as well.

"So unless someone like me, who was upset about the fact that the fireworks show would disturb the shelter's animals, killed the man, it's unlikely that the venue change was the motive behind what happened to the guy," I said.

"I wouldn't go so far as to suggest that we should remove the change in venue as a possible motive, but I'm starting to think there was a lot more going on that needs to be looked at closely."

"Like the fact that Gloria Arlington was at the home of her brother-in-law just a short time before the whole place exploded."

"Exactly. I also think there might be a motive in other backroom deals Arlington had been making. In my mind, it seems at least possible that in addition to Everson Development, Arlington might have had a financial stake in other companies."

"Since he owned shares in Everson Development, I guess that might suggest he'd invested in other companies along the way," I agreed. "And while we still don't know the details, the money deposited into Idlewild Development's bank account seems to suggest there were kickbacks at play."

"I've been working on following the money to see where it leads. So far, I haven't found a smoking gun, but I'll keep working on it." Tony turned back toward his computer and began saving everything before shutting down. "How about we take a break and have a virgin cocktail on the deck. I'm sure the dogs need to go out, so maybe the best plan is for the entire family to get some fresh air."

"That sounds good to me."

"I'm going to get you settled and then call Mike to give him another update. I know he was tracking down a few leads that may or may not have gone anywhere, but I know from experience that if I don't want to waste my time, I need to stay up to speed."

"I suppose it would be a waste of time to chase a financial trail for a suspect Mike has already cleared."

"It would. I'll bring my cell phone and a notepad and pen outside with me so we can be together. Hopefully, it will be a short call, and we can get on with the relaxation phase of our evening."

Of course, as I should have expected, Tony's call to Mike didn't turn out to be a short one. Not that I wasn't happy that both men seemed to be making progress since I really did want to get the case closed so I would no longer be labeled a person of interest in a murder investigation.

After Tony hung up with Mike, I asked him what they had discussed.

"Apparently, Mike received an anonymous call this morning. A male caller told Mike that he was on his way to meet with Arlington about a business matter when he received a call from a woman telling him that Arlington had been delayed and wanted to meet at the chamber's office rather than at his home as had been the original plan. The anonymous caller told Mike that the chamber's office was locked up tight, and no one appeared to be on the premises when he arrived, so he just headed home. When the man heard about the explosion later, he wondered if perhaps the woman who'd called him had known what was going to happen and had warned him off."

"So the suggestion here is that whoever set the fire knew that Mike's caller planned to be at the house, and not wanting him to die in the blast, she called him off."

Tony nodded. "That appears to be the case."

"So why didn't this anonymous caller identify themselves, and why didn't they call before this?"

Tony shrugged. "I'm not sure. Mike isn't sure, except that he suspects the man might know more than he's saying and doesn't want to get involved."

"That means that the person who set the fire must be a local. I know we suspected that the sister-in-law might have wanted to collect what she considered to be hers and set the fire when Arlington blew her off, but someone from out of state wouldn't have known about the meeting at Arlington's home or how to get ahold of the man who was called and redirected."

"That's exactly what Mike and I discussed earlier. We also feel that the anonymous caller must have known the arsonist."

"Someone like a member of the chamber's board or maybe a member of the chamber's staff," I said.

Tony nodded once again. "The theory is that both the woman who called to redirect the man who called Mike as well as the man who made the call to Mike were affiliated with the chamber in some way. This also explains why the man who contacted Mike didn't provide a name."

"He wanted to protect the woman who'd called him. Doesn't Mike at least suspect who the caller might be? Didn't Mike recognize the man's voice? If we're correct and the caller is either on the chamber's board or one of the chamber's staff members, then there are only so many people he can be."

"The caller intentionally disguised his voice, but Mike is looking into it. When I spoke to him earlier, he wanted to know if I had voice recognition software. I told him I have a program and could try but would need a sample to compare it to, so Mike plans on talking to every male associated with the chamber. He'll record the interviews, and we'll have our samples. If none of those match, we'll widen the search. At this point, we don't know if there is a link to the chamber. I mean, it's possible that the caller was the arsonist, and he lied about a woman calling him to throw us off."

I supposed that was true. If the guy was legit, it seems as if he would have left his name and contact information. The fact that he hadn't was suspect in my book.

"Did Mike say anything else?" I asked.

"Just that he's worried about you getting involved and potentially getting into a situation where you or Kiwi could be injured. He made me promise to keep an eye on you, which I already planned to do."

"I'll be careful," I said. "I promised not to go off sleuthing without you, and I won't. I had a nice nap, and now I plan to sit with Tilly and watch the sun go down. Maybe we can bring something out here for dinner."

"I have leftover pasta salad and can make hot sandwiches."

"That sounds perfect. We'll relax and get a good night's sleep, and then we'll go to my doctor's appointment tomorrow and find out if Kiwi is a boy or a girl."

"Still neutral?" Tony asked.

I took a minute to consider his question. "Actually, I am neutral, but I'm also curious."

He smiled. "Me too. I'll run in and grab the food, and then we'll eat. I was thinking about making Italian sandwiches with ham, salami, pepperoni, and mozzarella broiled in the oven and then topped with lettuce, tomato, and Italian dressing, served on one of the fresh rolls we bought at the bakery. Is there anything you don't want on it?"

"No. That sounds good, but toss a few sliced olives on my sandwich as well."

"Okay. I'll be back in a few."

After Tony left, I got up and walked toward the lake. All three dogs trailed along behind me. I loved our little piece of heaven and couldn't imagine moving into town. The baby wouldn't be starting kindergarten or even preschool for years, so it wasn't like we had to make any decisions right away, but the idea was there in the back of my mind that there would come a time we'd need to take a serious inventory of several aspects of our lives, including our living space.

Tony had suggested that we keep the lake house as a weekend getaway, which was a viable possibility. Tony did well with his software business, and the project he just completed with Zak Zimmerman would earn him even more. It wouldn't be out of the realm of possibility to have a home in town near schools and friends and another one here on the mountain where we could get away from the daily hustle of our lives.

Placing a hand on my stomach, I began to massage my baby circularly. Tony had urged me not to stress over these sorts of decisions until we needed to, and I knew he was right. This was my time to bond with my baby. For the next five months, he or she would be with me during every moment of every day, and I didn't need to share the baby with anyone, so I wanted to make the most of this one-on-one time we had together.

Tony came out with the food and began setting the outdoor table. I called the dogs to follow me and started back. I knew that Tony was as excited to meet our baby as I was, but in a way, I felt like I was already getting to know him or her. Not that I knew if the baby would have light hair or dark, or be outgoing and active or quiet and more of a homebody, but I knew that the baby didn't like hot mustard and that as he or she grew and became active, I'd have the opportunity to get to know the baby's rhythm long before the baby made his or her entrance into the world.

"Those look really good," I said, sitting across from Tony. "I've been thinking about our discussion relating to gender-neutral names, and I realized that while there are a lot of names that would be classified as gender-neutral, I tend to associate most names more strongly with one gender over the other."

"I guess that's natural. Does that mean you want to wait and see if we are having a boy or girl and then decide?"

"Not necessarily. Although if we do decide here and now before we know as we discussed, then I guess we need to reserve the right to change the name if we change our minds later."

"Agreed. How about Jordan after Michael Jordan or Peyton after Peyton Manning."

"I like both names, but I'm not naming my baby after a sports figure."

"Okay, then how about Parker after Peter Parker or Harley after Harley Quinn."

I rolled my eyes. "Same answer. I like the names, but if my baby is named after someone, it will be someone other than a comic book character."

Tony smiled the crooked little smile that let me know he was messing with me. "Lennon after John Lennon or Sawyer after Sawyer Brown."

I just looked at him.

"Drew, Frankie, Charlie, or Alex."

"I actually like Alex and Charlie, but Zak and Zoe have those names wrapped up."

"You know," Tony said, taking my hand in his, "we could just wait to name the baby until we meet him or her. That's the only way to really know if the name fits."

I smiled. "Actually, I love that idea. We can start a list, so we have a few ideas, but meeting our baby before we name him or her does seem to be the best idea either of us has had."

Chapter 9

I didn't think I would be nervous about having the ultrasound, but for some reason, I was. I supposed it could have been the dream I'd had the previous evening, which had quite honestly scared the bejeebers out of me. In my dream, I was tied to a table in a sparsely furnished room while a man in a white lab coat ran the ultrasound wand over my greatly enlarged stomach. When the image of my baby came on the screen, not only did it have a disfigured form, but it had bright yellow eyes that seemed to stare back at me. It was true that Tony and I had watched a horror movie not all that long ago where a human woman had been impregnated with a demon baby, so I supposed I knew how the imagery had made it into my subconscious. Dreaming about demon babies was something I hadn't had to worry about in the past, but now that I was expecting, I made the firm decision that there would be no more horror movies for this mama-to-be until my sweet little angel was safely delivered and nestled in my arms.

"Are you excited to meet your baby?" the ultrasound tech asked as she set up the 3D machine.

"Uh, sure," I replied.

"Are you hoping for a boy or girl?" the woman asked.

"Either is fine as long as he or she is human and doesn't have yellow eyes."

The technician looked at Tony.

He shrugged. "Horror movie that fed into a nightmare." Reaching down, he grabbed my hand with his, which I squeezed tightly.

"Ah," she said as she began to run the wand over my stomach.

"Is that my baby?" I asked as I pointed to the screen. Truth be told, with the big head, he or she did look a bit like an alien.

"That is your baby, and it looks as if everything is developing nicely."

"No yellow eyes?"

She smiled. "I can't tell eye color at this point, but given the fact that you and your husband both have brown eyes, I'm going to guess brown and not yellow."

"She's so cute," I said as I glanced up at Tony in time to see him swipe a tear from his cheek.

"She's perfect," he whispered.

"I think she's going to be a beauty," the technician agreed.

"She looks so real," I said in awe.

The woman laughed. "I can assure you she is quite real, right down to the little button nose."

"It looks like she's sucking her thumb," I said, pointing toward the screen.

Tony leaned in and took a closer look at the screen. "It really does look as if she might be." He turned and looked at the ultrasound tech. "I know we've been calling the baby she, but is she a girl, or is he a boy? It's hard to tell."

"She is most definitely a girl," the technician confirmed.

"A hundred percent for sure?" I asked.

"I'm not supposed to say that I'm one hundred percent sure, but I've been doing this a long time, and I've never been wrong."

"A princess for Daddy," I said, wiping away the tears running down my cheeks.

Tony leaned down and kissed me on the forehead. "A princess for both Mommy and Daddy."

"I'm going to take a couple of photos that I'll print so you can take them with you," the technician said. "Your doctor will talk to you about the ultrasound and answer any questions or concerns you might have, but it looks like everything is right on track."

Once the ultrasound tech finished doing what she needed to do, she instructed me to get dressed. I had an appointment with my doctor later that morning, but we had some time before we needed to be at the OBGYN's office, so I decided we should head to the diner and give my mom the good news. I felt a little bad that I hadn't told her about the baby right away and hoped that my telling her the news about the baby's gender would help to make up for that.

"Tess, darling, how are you?" Mom greeted me the minute Tony and I walked into the diner.

"I'm fine," I answered as Aunt Ruthie crossed the room and wrapped her arms around me.

"Your mom shared your news," Ruthie said. "I'm so happy for both of you."

"Thank you, Aunt Ruthie." I took Mom's hand in mine. "Tony and I stopped by because we wanted to let you know that we were at the hospital this morning so I could have an ultrasound."

"Is the baby okay?" Ruthie asked.

"She is," I answered.

"I'm so happy to hear that," Aunt Ruthie said. "Back in my day, they only did ultrasounds if they suspected some sort of a problem."

"I think everyone has one or more now," I said.

"She?" Mom asked. "Are we having a she?"

I nodded. "We are having a she."

Mom took her turn to wrap me in a hug. "I'm so excited for both of you," she said. "Have you picked out a name?"

"Not yet," I replied. "In fact, Tony and I have discussed waiting until we meet the baby before we name her, but we may change our mind again before she arrives."

"Have you told Bree?" Mom asked.

"No. We wanted to tell you first."

"Oh, honey." Mom hugged me again, and this time, there were tears with the hug. "That means a lot to me."

"I'm sorry I didn't tell you about the pregnancy sooner, but for some reason, I just needed time to adjust before I brought anyone in on the news."

"I understand," Mom said. "News of a first baby can be a big adjustment. A few days ago, I ran into an old friend who reminded me I was four months along with Mike before I filled my mother in."

Okay, wait. Old friend? What old friend? The fact that she admitted that she'd spoken to an old friend about my pregnancy a few days ago seemed to confirm that she already knew my news by the time I'd shared it with her. But as far as I knew, no one other than Zak and Zoe, Mike and Bree, and, of course, Brady and the guys from the county sheriff's office knew the secret. I'd been sure that Bree had been the one who filled Mom in, but Bree said she hadn't shared my news with Mom. Besides, would

Bree know that Mom hadn't shared her pregnancy news with her mother until she was as far along as I was now? If not Bree, could it have been Mike? I supposed it was possible that Mom might have shared the details of her pregnancy with Mike at some point, but the way she said "old friend" when referring to her reminiscence aid didn't fit with Mike being the person who helped her remember her past.

"So you ran into an old friend," I said.

"I did. A few days ago." She glanced toward Ruthie. "I'll have to tell you all about it, but not now. Ruthie and I need to get back to work."

"Okay," I said. "Tony and I need to go anyway. We want to tell Mike and Bree our news before my appointment with my doctor, but we'll get together soon."

"Okay, dear. Just give me a call and let me know what works for you. Now that Ruthie and I have decided to close at two, I'm finding that I have much more flexibility in my schedule."

"Do you think Mom ran into Dad?" I asked Tony the moment we left the diner.

"I would think that your mom would be a lot more upset than she appears to be if she had run into your father and if, after running into him, your mom realized who he was, but based on what was said and the way she said it, I think we need to at least consider the possibility."

"If it was Dad who reminded Mom about the pregnancy secret she kept from her own mother, then when did she run into him, and why didn't Mike say something?"

"Maybe Mike didn't know."

"If it was Dad who Mom ran into, and Dad knew about the baby, then it had to be Mike who told him. No one other than you, Bree, or I could have told him, and I know you and I didn't."

We shared our news with Mike and Bree on Friday, and we spoke to Mom on Monday, so I supposed that if Mom ran into someone who shared the news with her ahead of our announcement, it must have been on Saturday, Sunday, or early in the day before we visited her on Monday. Dad had been popping in on Mike every now and then, so it seemed possible to me that Dad had been in town to say hi to Mike and Ella, and while he was in town, he'd happened to run into Mom. The idea that Mom had realized who he was, had processed that information and seemed to have moved on from it didn't really work for me. In my mind, if Mom ever found out about Dad's undead state of being, she would surely blow a gasket, which ultimately would blow up her life. Instead, whatever had happened in the past few days seemed to have brought her a level of contentment and acceptance that I hadn't witnessed from her in a very long time.

"Did you tell Dad that Tony and I are expecting?" I asked Mike the moment Tony and I walked into his office.

His sheepish expression seemed to say it all. "I didn't think you'd mind. He came by to spend some time with Ella and me Saturday morning, and since I'd just found out about the baby the previous day, I figured he didn't know, so I mentioned it. He was overjoyed with the news, by the way."

I closed my eyes, blew a long breath out, and willed myself to relax.

"Are you mad?" Mike asked.

"Mad, no. It's fine. You were excited by the news and wanted to share it with Dad. But I think Mom ran into Dad when he was here, and I'm pretty sure she knows everything."

Mike's brows shot upward. "What? Why do you say that? Dad would never be so careless."

"I don't know anything with a degree of certainty, but Tony and I stopped by the diner to tell Mom we were having a girl. I wanted to tell her first since I felt bad about waiting so long to tell her about the pregnancy. Mom mentioned that she'd run into an old friend a few days ago who reminded her that she had waited until she was four months along to tell her mother that she was expecting when she was pregnant with you."

"And you think that old friend was Dad?"

I shrugged. "Who else would it be? I hadn't told Mom about the baby yet, so the only way she'd know that I was pregnant was if someone who knew my secret let it slip. Besides Tony and me, only you and Bree knew. Did you tell Mom?"

"No. Of course not. I wouldn't do that. But Bree might have if she thought it would help smooth things out between you and Mom."

"Did Bree know that Mom didn't share her first pregnancy with her own mother until she was four months into her pregnancy?"

"No. I don't think so. I'd never heard that story, so I couldn't have told her."

"We need to ask Bree if she knew," I said. "Maybe Mom told her at some point along the way."

"Bree is at the bookstore. Let's go and ask her. I'll let Frank know I'm going to take a break."

Bree was alone when we arrived at the bookstore. Mike turned the open sign to closed before announcing that we needed to talk. Poor Bree looked terrified until Mike explained what we needed to talk about.

"No," Bree said. "I hadn't heard your mom's story, and I certainly didn't tell her about the baby before Tess and Tony did. I thought about doing so for the very reason that you suspected, but I didn't."

"Then it had to be Dad who Mom spoke to," I said, suddenly feeling dizzy and suggesting we all head into the back room and sit down.

"The only one who knows for sure who your mother talked to is your mother," Tony pointed out. "I think we need to very carefully ask her."

"But if it wasn't Dad and it was a random friend who somehow knew that I was pregnant and that

Mom had waited four months to share the same news with her mother, she's going to think that it's odd that we asked," I said.

Tony just looked at me. "Random friend?"

"Yeah," I admitted. "I'm grasping." I put my hands on my head. At that moment, I was pretty sure I was losing my mind, and I knew I couldn't afford to do that.

"The diner wasn't busy," Tony said. "I could tell that your mom wanted to say more than she did, but Ruthie was standing close by, so she kept her comments to herself. If we call her and tell her that we're with Bree and Mike at the bookstore and want to talk to her about something predictable, maybe the party, perhaps she will suggest taking a break and joining us."

"That's a good idea," Mike said. "If Mom knows something and wants to talk, she'll make an excuse to join us."

As it turned out, Mom responded to Mike's call by suggesting she would take a break and join us.

In the five minutes it took for Mom to arrive, my mind went crazy with thoughts and images of all the possible ways this conversation might go. Tony tried to get me to relax, but as hard as I tried, doing so felt like an impossible task.

Once Mom arrived and joined us in the office, she immediately began speaking. "Before anyone says anything, I'd like to say something." She looked at me. "Yes, it was your father who told me about the baby, and yes, it is true that when I became upset that you hadn't told me yourself, Grant reminded me about the secret I kept from my mother for an equally long amount of time."

"Wait," I said. "You run into your dead husband, and the first thing you do is talk about your pregnant daughter?"

She laughed. "No, of course not. Let me back up."

"Backing up a bit would be good," Mike said, sounding as stunned as I was.

Mom very calmly began her story. "I was on my way to the diner early Saturday morning since I was scheduled to open that day so Ruthie could visit her grandchildren, who were involved in an event she wanted to attend. I was on my way into town when I realized I had Ella's bag in the car from her visit the previous day, and I decided I'd drop it off on my way to work. I figured I'd leave it on the porch if Mike and Bree weren't up and then text Mike to let him know it was there. When I arrived at their home, I noticed a light was on in the back of the house, so I headed toward the back door. I took a peek in the window and saw Mike having coffee with your father."

"Didn't you assume it was Uncle Garret?" I asked.

"I did," Mom answered. "For about a minute. And then he laughed, and I knew."

"You didn't come in," Mike said.

"No," Mom agreed. "I didn't come in. I was frozen in disbelief, trying to make sense of the sight before me. I watched for a few minutes as Grant cuddled with Ella while he spoke to you, and then I went back to my car. I needed to process things before I did whatever I would eventually do, but Grant walked around from the back of the house and headed down the street while I was processing things. I decided to follow him. Of course, he noticed me following him, and when he realized who it was, he stopped and waited for me to catch up. When I called him by name, he suggested we talk, so we went to my house. I called the waitress I had planned to work with that day and told her I was sick and Ruthie was otherwise occupied. I asked her to put a sign in the diner's window saying we'd reopen on Monday since we're closed on Sundays anyway."

"And then?" I breathed. I was sitting on the edge of my seat by that point.

"And then I asked Grant point blank how it was that he had been visiting with our son and granddaughter when the rumor was that he was very much dead, and he explained everything."

I glanced at Mike, who looked as shocked as I felt. "And?" I asked.

"And we had a very nice chat. Once we got the whole *"what he did and why he did it"* thing out of the way, he asked how I was. I shared a few things and asked him about his life, and he did the same. I asked him how long you and Mike had known the truth, and he shared the story, including the details leading up to him being at your house on the day I walked in unannounced. I shared with him that I never really bought the story about Uncle Garret, even though my mind insisted that it was the only explanation that made sense, and he shared that he sensed that I had my doubts. We talked all day, and once we got the specifics out of the way, we began to share other news. He made a comment at one point about how happy he was to be expecting two more grandbabies, and when I shared that I hadn't known about yours, he tried to smooth things over by reminding me that I'd done the same thing with my own mother when I was pregnant with Mike."

"And?" I asked again. I realized I kept asking that, but I was still waiting for the other shoe to drop.

"And nothing. Grant and I talked until it was dark, and then I offered to let him sleep on the sofa. He declined my offer but expressed relief and joy that he would no longer need to keep his secret from me. We hugged, and he left, but not before promising to stop by the next time he was in town to visit with you kids. It took all of Saturday night to process things. I called Sam on Sunday, he came over, and we talked. He filled in some of the blanks, and that is that."

"That is that?" I said in a voice that was much too squeaky.

She smiled. "I don't think I ever fully accepted the explanation I was given when your dad died, or I guess when he faked his death. Having answers to at least most of my questions has provided me with a level of peace and contentment that I haven't felt in a very long time. Grant is a good man. He is the father of my children and the grandfather of my grandchildren. I'm extremely grateful and happy that he didn't die in that fiery crash, and I'm extremely pleased that he'll be part of our lives. Of course, he'll need to be part of our lives as Uncle Garret so he doesn't blow his cover, but I'm fine with that."

"And Sam?" Mike asked.

"Sam knows the truth. I guess he always has. Nothing is going to change. I have a bond with your father that can never be broken, but I love Sam. I'm honestly not sure if I ever really loved your father, not the way I love Sam, but I did and do care about him. I think the three of us will be able to coexist just fine."

Talk about mind-blowing. I'd imagined hundreds of times how things might go if Mom ever found out about Dad, but calm acceptance was never in the equation. Maybe I hadn't given her enough credit. She had experienced a life that was both full and interesting. She seemed to be the sort to roll with the punches, at least until recently, and I guess I should have remembered that. If seeing Dad at the house had caused her mind to fragment between what she knew to be true and what could and could not be true, given the reality of Dad's past, then that might explain some of her erratic behavior as of late.

Mom crossed the room and hugged me. She then turned and hugged Mike. "I want you both to know that I really am fine. I've been struggling with the best way to tell you that I know what I know since your dad wasn't sure how you'd both take it, but I want to assure you that I really am fine. Better than fine. Happy and relieved. Not only do I understand the stakes, but I also understand that we all have opened ourselves to risk by allowing Grant into our lives. I've spoken to Sam, and in his opinion, now that your dad has retired, we should be able to actually be a family as long as we don't let our guard down and are very careful to keep our visits with Grant private."

"Dad retired?" I asked.

Mom nodded. "I guess I thought you knew. I suppose I should qualify that by saying that according to Sam, one can never really retire from the organization they both once worked for. But Sam has assured me that after he retired, changed his name, and dropped off the grid, he has been able to live a fairly normal life, and with time, Grant should be able to do so as well."

Wow. And I thought the big news of the day was the fact that Tony and I were having a girl.

"My doctor's appointment," I said to Tony. "We're going to be late."

"Not if we hurry."

"I want to finish this conversation, but I need to run. Can you all come to our place for dinner tonight?" I asked.

Everyone agreed they could, and I suggested Mom bring Sam as well. He would be instrumental in ensuring we did everything necessary to keep Dad off the radar. It would be harder for Dad to disappear since he had been active more recently, and he'd been at it longer than Sam had, but the fact that Sam actually led a relatively normal life gave me hope that maybe, with enough time, Dad would be able to as well.

Chapter 10

Tilly was waiting for Kiwi and me to take our afternoon nap. Until a few weeks ago, when we'd returned from Ashton Falls, I'd never been much of a nap person, but then I hit a point in my pregnancy where daily naps were the order of the day. While I did what I needed to do to ensure optimal health for myself and my child, I planned to cut out the naps once my body no longer craved them. At least, that had been my plan until I saw how much Tilly treasured that time when it was just the two of us, and Kiwi, of course, cuddled up on the bed. Maybe naps were going to be a permanent part of my life. At least as long as I had Tilly. I didn't like to think about the fact that she was getting older, but aging and eventually crossing the rainbow bridge was part of everyday life, and I knew that I'd ultimately need to accept that.

Of course, Tilly was a breed that tended to live longer than some other breeds, and I'd been careful to ensure her optimal health, so hopefully, she'd be around to watch Kiwi grow up, and like Tilly and me, Tilly and my baby would end up being the best of friends.

By the time I got up from my nap, Mike and Bree had arrived with Ella.

"Hey, sweetie," I said to Ella, picking her up and settling her on my hip. "How are you today?"

"Swim." She pointed toward the lake.

"The lake isn't really a swimming lake, but I have cookies inside." I looked at Bree. "If it's okay with Mommy, that is."

"One cookie is fine, but only one. Are the cookies homemade?"

I nodded. "Tony made sugar-free oatmeal cookies. I think he used applesauce instead of sugar. He's been more into healthy eating since he realized we were expecting."

"Sugar-free oatmeal sounds really good," Bree said. "Mommy will have a cookie as well."

I turned and headed back toward the house with Ella. Bree followed along.

"Where are the guys?" I asked as I set Ella down so that I could fetch the cookies.

"Mike wanted to talk to Tony about the case he's working on, and Tony had something to show him, so they headed down to the computer room. I was promised it would be a short detour, so hopefully, they won't be long."

I laughed. "Have you met Mike and Tony?"

She smiled. "Yeah, I've met them, and it is true that they'll likely become sidetracked, and we'll need to go and fetch them. So, how did your doctor's appointment go?"

"It went fine. Tony and I were ten minutes late, but the doctor was twenty minutes behind schedule, so it worked out okay."

"A girl," she said. "The news your mom shared about her and your dad not only meeting up but talking for hours was pretty distracting, and we never had the chance to discuss your news. How are you feeling about things?"

I smiled, placing a hand on my stomach. "I'm thrilled. Tony is thrilled as well. I'm sure Tony and I would have been just as happy if Kiwi was a boy, but having a girl somehow feels just right."

"You do realize that your baby is bigger than a kiwi now, don't you? You may have to settle on a different name."

"I saw my baby, and I know how big she is, but she's been Kiwi for so long that until we settle on an actual name, I think I'll just stick with what seems to be working."

"Do you have any name ideas?" Bree asked.

"We've tossed around a bunch of names but haven't settled on anything. In fact, we're leaning toward waiting until we've met our baby before we name her."

"I know that many people do that, but it adds a lot of pressure to the situation. Not that I'm saying you shouldn't do it that way, but it can be stressful to be handed the birth certificate paperwork and have no idea what to write on the line asking for the baby's name."

"I guess you make a good point," I admitted. "But Tony and I have time to figure it out. I'm not due for five months. Did you and Mike ever settle on a name for your baby boy?"

Bree looked down and smiled. "I think we are going to name him Michael after his daddy. We'll call him Michael rather than Mike, so there won't be confusion or a need for the junior/senior titles. I wasn't sure at first that I wanted to have a son with the same name as his father, but the more I thought about the idea, the more I liked it. At this point, we're undecided about the baby's middle name, but since Mike wants to loop your dad in, he's thinking about using Tucker. Michael Tucker Thomas."

"For Dad's alias of Grant Tucker." I paused and frowned. "Or maybe Grant Thomas is the alias, and Grant Tucker is his real name." My frown deepened. "You know, I have no idea what my father's actual name is, or I guess I should say what it was. The name he was given at birth. The name he grew up with."

"I guess you can ask him now that everything is out in the open," Bree suggested.

"I guess I can. So why Tucker? Why not Grant?"

Bree shrugged. "I asked Mike why he didn't just name him Michael Grant Thomas, and he said that he liked the name Tucker and felt like it was a better fit. I guess Michael Tucker Thomas does have a nice ring to it, although Mike will never be able to tell anyone that Tucker was to honor his father."

"Dad will know."

"That's the exact thing Mike said. I'm so glad things worked out okay with your mom. It has meant more to Mike that he's finally able to have a relationship with your father than I can say. After we discussed asking him to leave the area and not come back as a way of offsetting the Uncle Garret fiasco, I could see that Mike was not going to be okay with that. At first, I was very much against your father's early morning visits, but Mike is happier than I've ever seen him, and Ella loves her Dapa. She loves Gopa as well, and it seems that both Sam and your dad are completely okay with Ella having two grandpas who spend time with her on a regular basis."

"It's too bad your dad isn't around," I said.

"It is, but it is what it is." She took a bite of the cookie I'd handed her, and she'd only held to this point. "So what is Tony making for dinner? I'm starving."

"He's going to grill ribs and chicken. He also made pasta salad, green salad, fruit salad, and baked beans. I think he has bread to heat as well."

"That sounds really good."

"I can make a cheese and cracker platter if you want a snack. Dinner won't be ready for a while."

"A snack would be great. And maybe some of Tony's alcohol-free mojitos if you have the ingredients."

"He made a pitcher and left it in the refrigerator to chill. I'll pour us each a glass."

Mom and Sam showed up while Bree and I lounged on the deck with our beverages and snacks. I offered Sam a beer and Mom a glass of wine, but she decided on an alcohol-free mojito as well. I sent Sam downstairs to let Mike and Tony know they were here, and Mom joined Bree, Ella, and me on the deck.

"It really is just so lovely out here," Mom said. "I know I was making noise about flowers and decor for the party, but I don't think we need all that. The flower boxes you and Tony planted have added all the color we'll need. In fact, I think we should just keep it simple. We can grill some meat and then ask each guest to bring something to share. There really is nothing better than a good old-fashioned potluck."

The only thought that entered my mind was, *"Thank you, Dad, for helping Mom find her groove again."*

"I love that idea," I said. "Everyone we wanted to invite has been invited, so all we need to do is buy the meat and maybe the beverages."

"I'll bring a dessert," Bree said.

"And maybe Hap will make his cowboy beans," Mom said. "They truly are second to none other than your father's, of course."

"You know that Dad won't be able to come," I said, wanting to confirm that everyone was on the same page.

"I know, but we discussed having a family dinner with just Grant, you, Tony, Mike, Ella, Bree, Sam, and I here at your place where we have some privacy. Maybe later in the month."

"You spoke to Dad about dinner?"

"I did. I called Grant to let him know that he was going to have another granddaughter."

"Dad gave you his number?" Even I didn't have his phone number. Tony had a way of getting ahold of him, but a direct line would be great.

"He gave me a number to call if I needed him. When I call, I get an answering machine, and I'm supposed to ask if I reached Giuseppe's Pizza. Once I do that, I hang up. When Grant gets the message, he calls me back on the burner phone he gave me. Giuseppe's Pizza is the name of the pizza joint that was near the first little apartment we had together, so whenever he hears the name, he knows that it's me calling. Wasn't that smart of him to think of that?"

"It was smart," I agreed. I supposed that overall, I was happy that Mom and Dad had reconnected and found a way to be friends, but the whole thing was also really odd and would take some time to get used to.

"There they are," Bree said when Mike, Tony, and Sam all finally emerged from the house.

"Is everyone hungry?" Tony asked. "Should I start the meat?"

Everyone agreed they were hungry and that starting the meat was a great idea.

Mom, Bree, and I continued to chat while the guys got the food on the table. Once we were all seated and the food had been served, Mike brought up the subject we were here to discuss. He began the conversation by asking Sam what we needed to do to safely include Dad in our everyday lives. Since Sam had basically already done what Dad hoped to do, which was to find a way to live on the down low where ordinary lives went unnoticed, we asked him what to expect. He told us that Dad would be getting a new identity and look. I asked Sam what he meant by look, and he just smiled and assured us that whatever Grant came up with would be similar to his old style while being completely different at the same time. That statement made no sense to me. How could something be both similar and different at the same time? I wondered when Dad's retirement had actually taken place, and Sam informed us that while Dad had been working on the idea for a while, he hadn't made the decision to cut all ties to his agency and his old life until after the fiasco in December that had almost ended with his death.

"Your dad knows that he's past his prime, and the time has come to get out and blend in," Sam said.

"He did have a lot of facial hair when I ran into him," Mom said. "If I hadn't experienced a feeling of 'knowing' who was chatting with Mike, I wouldn't have recognized him if I'd simply run into him on the street. Well…" Mom paused, "except for his eyes. He has very distinctive eyes. I think the eyes were one of the main reasons the Uncle Garret explanation never really worked for me."

As we enjoyed the meal, we continued to throw out ideas that would allow us to welcome Dad back into the family. Sam had much more insight into the situation than we did, so I was pleased when everyone readily accepted his suggestions. Once dinner was over, Sam suggested that he and Mom head home, which Mom seemed happy to do. After they left, I took advantage of the opportunity to ask Mike about the case he and Tony had been working on.

"I feel like I'm missing something important," Mike said. "There seems to be no shortage of suspects, yet I can't quite seem to narrow things down."

"Maybe we can help. Who are you looking at?" I asked.

Mike leaned back on the sofa and began to share his thoughts. "I spoke to Bodine Cosgrove. If you remember, we found a text chain on Arlington's phone between Arlington and Bodine early on, which ended when Arlington instructed the man to call him on his other phone. Tony was able to track that other phone to Idlewild Development."

"I remember," I said.

"I figured that if Arlington had instructed the man to call him on his business line, Bodine likely had been engaged in some sort of business for that company, so I called and spoke to him about it. While Bodine wouldn't say anything specific which might implicate himself, he did confirm that he had reason to believe that Arlington could be bought."

"So for the right price, Arlington would not only push your agenda item through the chamber's board, but he would smooth things over with the town as well."

Mike nodded. "Basically. Cosgrove was careful not to be too specific when I spoke to him, but something he said led me to a man named Craig Holmes. Craig is the out-of-state contractor whose company is developing the housing development we discussed previously. Not the one near the animal shelter, but the one near the park."

"Did he tell you anything that might help narrow things down?" I asked.

"No," Mike said. "Not really. But when I asked him to provide a timeline of his interaction with Arlington, it occurred to me that we might be able to match town council votes with deposits into Idlewild Development. Orchestrating a comparison is what Tony and I were doing after Bree and I first got here. We found three cases where a controversial vote by the chamber led to a deposit into the Idlewild account the following day. All three chamber-approved projects were sent to the town and approved by the town as well."

"So what's your next move?" I asked.

"I plan to speak to the person in charge of these three projects tomorrow. I'm hoping someone will say something that leads to a motive for murder."

"At this point, I suppose that an individual who completed a successful transaction with Arlington and ended up with what they were after wouldn't necessarily have a motive to kill the man."

Mike agreed with my assessment.

"I still think the method of death is important," Bree said. "I mean, why blow up the whole house and risk the fire spreading to the forest or other properties if the fact that the man died due to his proximity to fireworks isn't important."

"Bree has a point," I said. "I mean, why not shoot the guy or poison his drink. Why do something so grand unless the method of death was as important as the death itself."

"Which brings me back to you as a suspect," Mike pointed out.

I supposed that was true.

"What about other members of your protest group?" Mike asked. "The photo I saw featured at least ten individuals picketing Arlington's real estate office."

"Most of the picketers are animal shelter volunteers or friends and family of the shelter's volunteers," I answered. "I don't think there was a single person in that group who would kill the man." I looked at Tony. "Were you ever able to match the voice associated with the man who called Mike anonymously?"

"No. I can say that the voice doesn't match any member of the Chamber of Commerce, the town council, or the staff of either agency."

"What about a financial stake in Arlington's money-making scheme?" I asked. "Did you ever find anyone other than Arlington who seemed to be accepting the kickbacks?"

Tony and Mike both informed me that, to this point, it appeared as if Arlington was the only one who had been accepting bribes.

"It's getting late, and I'm getting tired," Bree said.

Mike assured her he'd wrap it up, and they could head home. I went upstairs to fetch Ella while Mike finished with Tony, and then Tony and I helped the little family to their car.

Chapter 11

Tony had a small amount of work to complete for one of his clients, but he assured me he'd be finished by lunch if I wanted to go into town. I responded by telling him that while I didn't have any appointments today, I had been feeling antsy, and lunch in town might help eliminate that. I also informed him that I was planning on puttering around in the garden this morning and might prefer a nap to lunch out by the time I started on that, so Tony suggested that we wait to discuss it after he was freed up, and I agreed.

The planter boxes around the patio had been finished over the weekend and really didn't need any attention, but the small bed where Tony had planted flowers to attract butterflies last summer needed to be trimmed and weeded. The perennials had returned, although they did need a bit of TLC, but the annuals near the front of the bed would need to be replaced once the weeds had been pulled, the old growth was trimmed, and the soil was tilled. I doubted I'd have the energy to finish the whole thing today, but I figured that if I got the bed started, Tony could pick up where I stopped and finish it.

I smiled at Tilly, who found a place in the shade where she curled up to watch me. Titan and Kody were chasing each other around the house time and time again. I laughed as they galloped by for the third time. Oh, to have that much energy.

When the dogs didn't return after they lapped the bed I was weeding for the fourth time, I stood up and looked around. "Titan," I called. "Kody."

I heard a happy yip coming from the forest that hugged the property line on the far side of the house, so I took my dirty gloves off and walked in that direction, intent on reminding the dogs to stay where I could see them.

"Dad," I said as I watched my father walking from the forest with both dogs walking by his side. Titan and Kody were usually protective of the property, but Dad came around often enough that the dogs knew him by this point. "I didn't realize you were in town."

He continued forward and then hugged me. "I've been around for a couple of weeks. I'm looking at cabins in the woods that are for sale, so I'll have a place of my own where I can stay when I'm visiting the area, which, with all the grandchildren to dote on,

I plan to do a lot more often. Congratulations on your daughter in the oven."

I automatically put a hand on my stomach. "Thank you. Tony and I are very happy." I looked around. "Are you sure you weren't followed?"

"I'm sure. You aren't expecting company, are you?"

"No. Tony is downstairs catching up on some work for a client, and I was working in the garden." I glanced down at Tilly, who had wandered over to stand by my side. "Can I get you something? Maybe something to drink or even a late breakfast?"

"Something cold to drink would be nice. I can't stay long, but I wanted to come by to congratulate you before I took off."

"Will you be gone long?" I asked as I turned and motioned for Dad and the dogs to follow me into the house. Tang hissed at Dad when he walked in, while Tinder just ignored him, and once Dad settled at the kitchen table, both cats ran up the stairs.

"I need to clean up some loose ends before I completely transition into retirement. I guess that might take a couple of months. Maybe even three. I hope to be back by the time Mike's baby is born in October. I missed so much with Ella. I want to be here for all the firsts experienced by Michael as well as all the firsts experienced by your daughter. Do you have a name yet?"

"Not yet. We're just calling our daughter Kiwi for now."

Dad smiled. "I seem to remember calling you Kiwi when we were expecting you. I think Mike was Melon."

I poured a tall glass of iced tea for both of us before I sat down at the table. "I spoke to Mom."

"I was wondering if you were going to bring all that up."

I wrapped my hands around my frosty glass. "Of course, I'm going to bring it up. Mom finding out that the husband she thought had been dead for more than two decades is alive is huge news."

"While our encounter was unplanned, I thought it went well considering."

"Yeah," I agreed. "Mom did seem to be eerily calm about things. In fact, she seemed to be much more calm and content than she's been for years. She told me that she always had questions about your death that she couldn't seem to find satisfactory answers for."

"Didn't you have the same questions, which caused you to look for me in the first place?" Dad asked.

"I did have questions, and those questions did prompt me to ask Tony to do some digging on my behalf."

Dad took a long drink of his tea. "If I had to do it over, I suppose I'd do things differently, but at this point, all we can do is move forward."

"Do you think spending more time in White Eagle will provide you with a way to move forward?"

He shrugged. "I guess I'm hoping as much."

"What about the danger to yourself and your family that you've told me about for years? Wasn't that the reason you did what you did in the first place? Is that danger going to simply evaporate?"

"No," Dad admitted. "Not entirely. I will be given a new identity that won't be linked back to my life as Grant Thomas, Grant Tucker, or any of my aliases in any way. I plan to change my looks, maybe a nose job or fuller lips. I even plan to change my voice. I know that simply stepping back into my old life won't be possible, but I'm hopeful my new identity will be convincing enough that I can spend time with you kids without anyone figuring out that Clark Houston is really Grant Thomas."

"Clark Houston?" I asked.

He shrugged. "I'm trying on new names. I was undercover as a cowboy for a while, so Clark from Texas is an option, but I'm also considering Bruce from Brooklyn or Thatcher from Tennessee, amongst others."

"I'm excited to see what you come up with. So, are you really going to have plastic surgery?"

"Like I said, I will have a few small changes made to sell the package."

"Don't forget the eyes. Mom said your eyes are very distinctive."

He smiled. "Did she now?"

I nodded. "Mom said that your eyes are the reason for her doubting that Uncle Garret was a brother and not her dead husband reincarnated. Maybe colored contacts would do the trick."

"I'll keep that in mind." He looked at his cell phone. "I really do need to go. I may not be back for a few months, so don't worry about me if I don't show up as often as I have been as of late."

"I'll be fine. Have you talked to Mike?"

"I have, and he understands."

"And Mom?"

"She knows how to contact me if she really needs me."

"You know, it might be a good idea to give Mike and me the same number you gave Mom."

He shook his head. "Not the same number, but maybe a different number. If you receive a burner phone in the mail in the next few weeks, you'll know it's from me." He stood up, and I stood as well. "Take care of Kiwi," he said, kissing me on the forehead. "Maybe she'll have a real name by the time I return."

"Maybe."

After Dad slipped out the back door, I headed downstairs to tell Tony about his visit. The whole thing had lasted barely ten minutes, but I was surprised to find that Dad hadn't wanted to speak to Tony as long as he was here. Maybe he meant to, but whatever message he received on his cell phone caused him to leave sooner than planned.

"You'll never guess who just stopped by," I said after I joined Tony in the clean room.

"Your dad."

"How did you know?"

He pointed to the monitors that allowed him to view the entire property, including the path from the forest to the house.

"I should have remembered that you had the entire yard outfitted with security cameras. If you knew Dad was here, why didn't you come up?"

"It looked as if he was here to visit with you. I didn't want to interrupt. I figured you'd come and get me if you needed me, but if this was a personal visit between father and daughter, I'd stay out of the way."

"Are you about done here?"

"I am," he answered.

"How about a drive?"

"Do you have a specific destination in mind?"

"I do." I paused. "I know I agreed to stay out of things, but I have an idea I want to check out."

Tony looked at me with suspicion in his eyes. "What sort of idea?"

"Let's just get ready, and I'll explain as you drive."

Of course, while Tony went along with things initially, once we got underway and I informed him that I wanted to drive by the lot where Arlington's home had once stood, he resisted. It took some persuading, but eventually, I got him to go along with my idea.

"What exactly are you looking for?" Tony asked me after I'd instructed him to pull over in front of Arlington's plot of land, and I exited the truck.

"I'm looking for a lie."

"A lie?"

I nodded. "I've been thinking about the neighbor who called and spoke to Frank. The one who told him that he'd seen an improperly parked BMW in the driveway in front of Arlington's home just before the explosion and assumed the sedan belonged to a woman since he'd heard a female voice coming from inside."

"I remember Mike telling us about the neighbor. He told Frank he'd been walking his dog and had just passed Arlington's home when he noticed the BMW in the driveway."

I nodded and looked around. "We're standing on the street in front of the location where the house stood before it exploded. I realize the house is no longer standing, but something feels off. Does it seem to you that a passerby would have been able to see either the house or the driveway from this vantage point?"

Tony furrowed his brow. "I see your point. The grove of aspens along the property line is fairly dense. It doesn't seem that anyone would have been able to see the house unless they walked onto the property and up the driveway a bit."

"Exactly." I walked down the street to the point where the driveway intersected with the street. The driveway curved toward the right after it cleared the grove. I was willing to bet that the only way the neighbor could see the BMW was if he'd walked up the driveway and made the turn.

"Maybe Frank has additional information about what was said during his conversation with the neighbor," Tony suggested. "Information Mike didn't pass on."

"Maybe we should call him," I suggested.

Tony agreed and pulled his cell phone out. While he made the call, I slowly stepped onto the property and followed the driveway toward the foundation where the house had once stood. Less than a minute later, Tony came jogging up to join me.

"Did you speak to Frank?"

"I did," Tony answered. "Frank said that the next-door neighbor to the right, a man named Elroy Gwen, called him shortly after the explosion and told him the story about walking his dog down the street past Arlington's home, seeing the car, and hearing the argument between Arlington and a female visitor. Frank said he had no reason to doubt Elroy since Elroy had called him and the man wasn't a suspect, so he took the information and then canvassed the area, looking for another resident who might have seen something. Initially, no one admitted to having seen anything, but then a man who identified himself as Dave called Frank on Monday morning and told him that he'd been out of town when Frank had been by and had just returned. He also told Frank that his neighbor told him he'd seen Frank going house to house looking for anyone who'd seen the BMW."

"Which Dave told Frank he had," I added.

Tony nodded. "As you remember, he told Frank that the sedan was a BMW, most likely an Eight Series, and that the license plate had been issued in Nevada. This led Mike and Frank to Gloria Arlington. When Gloria admitted that she'd been at the house and argued with Wilton before the explosion that killed him, they figured they had the verification they needed to suggest that Elroy had been telling the truth. Frank said they never did another thing to look into the man's story."

"And yet here we are with questions and inconsistencies."

"Here we are." Tony agreed.

"Although I do understand why Mike and Frank might not have considered it necessary to look into Elroy's story further once they traced the car back to the sister-in-law."

"I agree that it did seem like they had the whole story at this point." Tony looked around. "So if we think there is more to the story, what are we thinking? Are we thinking Elroy came up the driveway, saw the car, heard the argument, left, and then returned the way he came?"

I walked away from the debris where the house had once stood and toward the woods. "Did the house have security cameras in the driveway?"

"As a matter of fact, there was a camera on the post where the driveway meets the street. I noticed it when we were standing there."

"So if someone accessed the property via the driveway, the camera would have picked them up."

"Yes, I would say that would be the case."

I slowly entered the tree line from the clearing between the house and the woods, stood perfectly still, and looked around. I remembered someone, maybe Mike, telling me that the reason for deciding that the fire had been arson and not an accident was because they'd found part of a fuse in the woods across from the storage shed where the fireworks had been kept. If the fuse was found right about where I was standing, then it seemed at least possible that Elroy could have walked through the woods to Arlington's home without walking up the main driveway. I said as much to Tony.

"So you're suggesting that Elroy was the arsonist," Tony said. "He came through the woods with the idea of setting off the fireworks and destroying the home, but when he got here, he saw the car and heard the arguing. Elroy might not have wanted to harm an innocent person and waited for Gloria to leave. Maybe after he went home, he realized who Gloria was and decided that she might make a good red herring to draw the police from his trail, so he called Frank and told the story of the BMW in the driveway and arguing coming from the house. He may have intentionally refrained from sharing a lot of detail as a means to keep the whole thing casual."

"And then on Monday, when Mike and Frank still hadn't tracked Gloria down, Elroy calls back and gives them additional information, although this time he tells them his name is Dave. Mike and Frank have no reason to doubt the helpful neighbor, whose intel is correct, and they tracked down Gloria and don't look any closer at Dave."

Tony picked it up again. "And then Mike has the PD talk to Gloria, and they decide she might not have done it after all, but Elroy still needs a diversion to cement the case, so he calls back once again as an anonymous caller and tells Mike about the woman who called him about a change in the location of his meeting with Arlington. This puts Mike back on the track of looking for a woman as the killer."

"Okay, this works, but why did Elroy kill Arlington?" I asked.

Tony shook his head. "No idea. Maybe we should call Mike and let him figure it out."

"Not yet. All we really have at this point is a theory. We'll need some sort of proof." I started to walk through the woods. Tony called after me, but I ignored him, so he followed me. When I arrived at a brick wall that separated Elroy's property from the forest, I noticed a tool shed in one corner. I climbed over the short wall and headed toward the shed. I could hear Tony whispering for me to return to the truck and call Mike, but I ignored him.

"You wait here," I said when I arrived at the shed and found it unlocked. "If you see anyone coming, let me know."

With that, I slipped into the wooden building. The first thing I noticed was a workbench. The second thing I noticed was a roll of fuse sitting on the bench. Next to the fuse was a gas can. I opened the lid to the can to make sure there was gasoline or another accelerant inside before I called Mike with my suspicion. There was.

Gotcha, I thought to myself.

I'd just turned around to head back toward Tony when he walked into the shed with a tall man walking behind him. A tall man with a gun at Tony's back.

"I really hoped the two of you would leave this alone," the man said.

At that moment, I really wished that as well.

There was no doubt in my mind that the man didn't have anything pleasant in mind for Tony or me. I placed my hand on my stomach and thought about Kiwi. I really didn't think things through at that point. My urge to protect my child was overwhelming. Since I was standing next to the open gasoline can, I picked it up and lunged forward, sloshing gasoline toward Elroy's face. Luckily, my aim and the strength I put behind my task were right on. Elroy dropped the gun and then began to scream as he tried to get the gasoline out of his eyes. Tony knocked the man to the floor while I grabbed the gun. Once I had the gun trained on the man who would have done harm to my baby, Tony used rope that was hanging on the wall to tie the man's hands, and I took my cell phone out and finally called my brother, a move I was willing to admit, I should have simply executed in the first place.

Chapter 12

"I'm with you for most of this, but why did Elroy want to kill Arlington in the first place?" Bree asked after she joined me on the patio and sat in the lounge chair next to the one I was sitting on.

"Initially, I had no idea, but Mike got him to admit that Arlington had been setting off small explosions on his property for months. I guess the guy was more into fireworks than we thought. Apparently, the noise was driving Elroy's dog crazy, so when he asked Arlington to stop, and the man refused, he decided to blow up his stash."

"So he killed a man over fireworks?" Bree asked.

"According to Mike, Elroy thought the house was empty. He saw Arlington walk Gloria out of the house and thought Arlington went with her when she left. He only meant to destroy the fireworks, but, as it turned out, he caused a lot more damage than he anticipated."

"Wow. That's a crazy story."

"I feel somewhat bad for the guy," I said.

Bree looked me in the eye. "The man was going to kill you."

"Maybe, but he might not have. He never had the opportunity to figure out what to do with Tony and me. The moment I realized that Kiwi was in danger, I went crazy. I nearly blinded the guy."

"I don't think gasoline in the eye will blind you."

"Maybe not, but it sure looked like it hurt like heck."

Bree reached out and hugged me. "I'm just glad that both you and Kiwi are okay. The situation could have turned out a lot differently."

"It could have," I admitted. "Tony wanted to call Mike as soon as we had a new theory, which would have been the right move, but I wouldn't listen." I put a hand on my stomach. "I definitely need to learn to be a lot more careful. Not only am I eating for two, but I'm living for two. My life is not really mine to gamble with any longer."

"I'm glad you recognize that. Being a mom can be tiring and stressful, and you may have to give up some of the things you previously enjoyed, but it is totally worth it."

Mike, who had been working downstairs in the computer room with Tony, came outside. He sat down on a lounge chair next to Bree's.

"So, did you get everything wrapped up?" Bree asked.

"I did. Elroy has been turned over to the county office in Kalispell, and the officer in charge has been given all the evidence we've collected. The guy admitted to blowing up Arlington's home, but he's sticking to his story that he didn't mean to kill him. I'm not convinced he's telling the truth, but my job was to find and arrest him. It's up to the court and the attorneys to figure out the rest."

"In a way, I'm surprised it turned out to be the neighbor," Bree said. "I guess he came up a time or two during the investigation, but he was never considered to be a suspect." She looked at her husband. "At least not that you said."

"He wasn't even on my radar," Mike admitted. "Initially, I thought it was Tess."

"Hey," I complained.

Mike smiled and continued. "And then I was sure the killer was the sister-in-law. She really did seem to have a strong financial motive, and she had been overheard arguing with the man. After she was cleared, I was really gunning for someone who'd entered into a backroom deal with the man that went bad."

"What's going to happen with that anyway?" I asked. "It seems that the individuals who paid

Arlington to manipulate a vote should be punished in some fashion for their involvement."

"I don't disagree," Mike said, "but it isn't up to me. I gave a list of names and the transactions associated with the names to the district attorney, and I guess he'll need to decide whether or not to do anything with that list."

"Well, I'm just happy that this whole thing is over," Bree said. "Is Tony coming up? He did promise us dinner."

"He needed to make a call, but he'll be up in a few minutes," Mike assured Bree. "I'm going to go inside and grab a beer. Do you want anything?"

"There's a pitcher of non-alcoholic margaritas in the refrigerator," I said. "I'll take one over ice."

"And I'll have one as well," Bree seconded. She turned and looked at me after Mike left to fetch the drinks. "It's really nice of Tony to go out of his way to make sure we have something fun to drink."

"He's really into it," I said. "He's been working on mocktail recipes since we returned from Ashton Falls. Some haven't turned out the way he hoped, but most have been delicious. He made mai tais a few nights ago, which were really just a few types of fruit juice mixed in a tiki mug with fresh fruit garnish, but they were delicious."

"That does sound good. We'll have to ask Tony to make those next time."

Mike returned with the beer and mock margaritas. He'd just sat down when Bree looked up, turning her head slightly toward the house.

"It sounds as if Ella is up from her nap."

"I'll get her." Mike set his beer on the table next to the chair he'd just sat in and headed toward the house.

"I didn't even hear her," I said.

"You will when the crying baby is yours."

I hoped so. I supposed I'd need to depend on a baby monitor if I didn't develop Bree's super hearing once my little girl was born.

By the time Mike returned with a smiling Ella, Tony had finished his call and was on his way out to join us.

"Is everything okay?" I asked.

Tony smiled and then nodded. "Better than okay. That was Zak. I guess the software we came up with is a huge hit, and he has two other high-end customers looking for something similar yet personalized. He wanted to know if I would be interested in working with him again."

"Are you?" I asked.

He nodded. "I told him I wanted to think about it, but I think I am. Not only was the product Zak and I came up with unique and quite amazing, but Zak is such a nice guy. I had the best time working with him."

"Zak and Zoe are both pretty great," I agreed. "When do you have to let him know?"

"Zak's on the road trip he told us about with his family right now and won't be back for three more weeks, so he told me to think about it and that we'd talk when he got back."

"It sounds like you have plenty of time to think it over," Mike said.

"I do," Tony agreed.

"I'd like to meet Zak and Zoe," Mike said. "They sound like the type of people we'd get along with."

"Oh, they are," I agreed.

I jumped into a Zak and Zoe story, which I sensed Bree was less thrilled to hear than Mike was. Mike saw the potential in a business relationship between Zak and Tony, while I think Bree was a little jealous about the way I tended to go on and on about Zoe.

After catching myself in the act of gushing over Zoe and her remarkable life, I changed the subject and asked Tony if he'd been copied on the email I received from Tim and Tom, the Ghost Therapists, that morning.

"I did receive the email," he informed me. "It sounded like they planned to switch things up a little this year. I didn't have time to read the whole thing, so I'll need to look it over again when I have the opportunity."

"We had a raffle the last time they were here, and the winners were given tickets to spend the night in the haunted house with Tim and Tom, but it sounded like they plan to bring in professional actors this year. If the locals aren't allowed to participate, they'll be disappointed, but I suppose we'll need to go along with whatever arrangements the mayor already agreed to."

"When I was in junior high, I did a book report on the Stonewall Estate," Mike informed us. "The place has an interesting history. If the show works out the way the men hope, I imagine you'll have a decent television special."

Ella had been playing on a blanket on the grass while the four adults had been talking. She must have grown tired because, after a bit, she gave up on her play and crawled into Tony's lap. She leaned her head against his chest and popped her thumb in her mouth. Tony stoked her hair and began to rock slightly without losing a beat in the conversation. My heart melted a little as I watched Tony cuddle with his niece. The two had always had a special bond. In fact, any time Tony was around, he was the one she wanted to hold or help her. Tony really had a way with children, all children, but especially Ella. As I watched the pair gently rock. I had this overwhelming desire for December to hurry up and get here.

Chapter 13

July Fourth

By the time July fourth had arrived, life had settled into a calm routine. Don't get me wrong, hosting a party for more than sixty people was no small job, but the amount of prep work an event such as this demanded had been greatly reduced by the change from a host-prepared meal to a potluck meal.

"Your yard is lovely," Hattie said after she crossed the yard and joined me on the patio. "When Hap and I ran into you at the nursery and saw the flower combination you'd chosen, I knew it would be nice, but this is really spectacular."

"Thank you. I'm happy with the way things turned out. I'm sorry I haven't had the chance to come by and see your flowers, but it's been kind of crazy around here."

"I heard that you and Tony solved Wilton Arlington's murder."

I nodded. "I guess we did, but it was actually a team effort. Mike, Frank, and Gage did most of the groundwork that provided the puzzle pieces I needed to develop my theory." I laughed. "Actually, my idea to go to Arlington's place and check out the crime scene was less of a theory and more of a random thought I followed up on."

Hattie patted my hand. "I'm just glad you, Tony, and the baby came through it okay. Now that you're going to be a mama, it would be best for you to give up your sleuthing hobby."

"I agree. I was terrified for the baby when I realized that Tony and I were in real trouble. She has to be my number one priority. From now on, I'm leaving the detective work to Mike."

"That's my girl."

"So what are we talking about," Hap asked after he crossed the yard and joined Hattie and me.

"Babies," Hattie said.

"I noticed that you were talking to Angie," I said. "I wasn't sure if she was coming, but since she's here, I need to grab her so I can ask her about the electrical for the Ghost Whisperer episode Tim and Tom will be in White Eagle to tape in October."

"Given what they do, it seems that these men would have their own power," Hap said. "A generator to run their equipment."

"I think the guys have a generator they use when they don't have other options, but the last time the pair was in town, I remember that Tim and Tom wanted to tap into the electrical system of the haunted house they were featuring if possible. I imagine the guys may be limited in terms of the type and amount of equipment they can run at any one time if they're exclusively on generator power."

"I guess that might be the case," Hap agreed. "Will the town be auctioning off tickets to join the men during their overnight stay again?"

"I'm not sure. Initially, I heard that Tim and Tom didn't want an audience, but I spoke to Tony about it just this morning, and he said that he'd spoken to Tim on the phone yesterday and, according to Tim, the men do want to have amateurs on set. Tim believes that having a live audience makes things a bit more tense for the viewer. I agree with that. Tony does as well. At this point, Tony and I have agreed to get through this party and then look into it further. We have time to fine-tune the details, so Tony suggested we enjoy the party and deal with Halloween later."

"That sounds like fine advice," Hap agreed.

Hap and Hattie wandered over to talk to a group from the senior center where they occasionally spent time, and I headed into the house to check on the food that still needed to be set out. I'd been dreading this party since Mom first suggested it, but everything was going smoothly, and everyone appeared to be having a fantastic time. Not only had the workload been reduced with Mom's change in attitude, but the weather was nearly perfect. Sunny with a cloudless blue sky, but not at all hot as it often got on a July day.

"Fantastic party," Aspen said after she entered the kitchen from the yard. "The food is delicious, the drinks creative, and the yard gorgeous."

"Thank you. The food, yard, and creative beverages were all Tony, but I'm happy to take credit for marrying such a well-organized guy."

She smiled. "Tony really is the best. I hope I can find my Tony one day."

"Tony is one of a kind. There are, however, a few great guys in town who are still single. Brady, for instance."

She looked around the room, presumably to confirm that we were alone, and then she replied. "Brady is great. He's kind, thoughtful, and funny, and I can totally see us as a couple. I suspect Brady feels the same way, but taking that step from friendship to something more is a risk I'm not sure I am willing to take. He's my boss. If we tried dating, and it didn't work out. I'm afraid it would ruin our fantastic boss/employee relationship. I love my job, and I hesitate to engage in any activity that could potentially ruin what I already have."

"I get that. If I were in your shoes. I'd honestly feel the same way."

"So what should I do?" she asked. "Should I consider Brady off limits and just move on and look for another guy? Should I wait to see if Brady makes the first move toward a romantic relationship, and if he does, should I agree to take that step with him, or should I suggest we keep things professional?"

"That's something only you can decide."

"I realize that my relationship with Brady is ultimately between me and Brady, but I really could use some advice."

"Has there been a move on either of your parts toward taking the next step in your current friendship?"

"Not really. There have been a few times when we're chatting about something work-related, and from out of nowhere, I feel this pull. I think he feels it as well. But so far, we simply take a step back and then bring the conversation back into the work zone." She took a deep breath. "I've thought about this a lot, and I'm no closer to figuring out what to do. On the one hand, as I said, I love my job and would hate to do anything that would ruin the easy relationship Brady and I currently have. But on the other hand, am I taking a risk that Brady truly is the perfect guy for me, and if I pass up my chance with him, will I miss out on the opportunity for the best thing in my life?"

I reached out and gave Aspen a hug. "I can't tell you what to do, but I will say that if it were me and I really thought that Brady was the one, I'd go for it. There are other jobs if the situation you fear does come to pass, but I doubt there are many other guys as perfect for you as the one you currently have."

Aspen smiled. "Thanks, Tess. That really does help."

I watched Aspen cross the yard. She headed toward Brady, who was chatting with Mike. I watched as Brady noticed her and then smiled. I recognized that smile. Tony looked at me exactly that way. I really wasn't sure if a relationship between Aspen and Brady would go the distance, but I hope it did. They were both exceptional people, and I really loved it when the people in my life who meant the most to me were as settled and happy as I was.

USA Today best-selling author Kathi Daley lives in beautiful Lake Tahoe with her husband Ken. When she isn't writing, she likes spending time hiking the miles of desolate trails surrounding her home. Find out more about her books at **www.kathidaley.com**

Made in the USA
Coppell, TX
21 June 2024

33734094R10095